The Scooter Chronicles

A Southern California **MOD**yssey

Shahriar Fouladi

Burger Music Publishing

Printed in China.
First printing, 2018

www.burgerrecords.com

Designed by Larry Renac

Publisher: Ted Adams

ISBN: 978-1-68405-185-4

Published and distributed by IDW Publishing, a division of Idea and Design Works, LLC, under license from Shahriar Fouladi and Burger Music Publishing. The IDW logo is registered in the U.S. Patent and Trademark Office.

Contents

ACKNOWLEDGEMENTS

My life has taken a lot of weird turns and there are a lot of people to blame. I have to start with Bart Mendoza, who helped assemble a lot of the cool extras in this book, such as the soundtrack songs, the essay, and the photos. His expertise on the Southern California Mod scene is second to none.

Next, I would like to thank Matt Hoffman for helping put this little book together and for always being the voice of reason.

A big thanks to Larry Renac for designing the cover and adding some really cool design touches to the book, particularly the photo section.

I'd like to express my appreciation for the very talented Ralph Cosentino, whose great *Victor the Vespa* drawing blew me away.

I'd like to thank my parents, Flora and Ali, and my two sisters, Zarnaz and Sarvenáz, for always encouraging me and believing in me as I followed my dreams. I'd also like to express my appreciation for some of the other friends and family members who have been a big part of my life: David, Lisa, Darius, Victoria, Faye, and Viola.

Last, but certainly not least, I'd like to acknowledge the role of my wife Laura, who is the best editor and the most thoughtful person I've ever met. Thanks for being my conscience and my biggest supporter every day.

Is this really how I'm going to die?

Tommy asks himself this question, as he runs for his life through a massive grassy field. He hears footsteps getting closer and closer.

Sprinting faster than he ever has before, Tommy enters an area covered with winter creeper plants. His foot gets caught on the plants and he tumbles over. He pulls his foot with all his strength. He'd chew it off if he could. Just as he's about to extricate himself, he looks up. It's too late.

The mad man stands there smiling and pointing his rifle directly at Tommy.

"Too bad. You lose, man."

Tommy stands up. He wants to plead for his life, but no words come out. He closes his eyes. He flashes back to his life as it was two weeks ago: He had a hot girlfriend, less than a month until he started college, and the money to buy the Vespa of his dreams. And now, he faces what are probably his final moments on Earth.

A loud bang. Tommy feels a burning pain in his stomach. He opens his eyes and looks down.

All he sees is red . . .

PART 1: MOD ROLLERCOASTER

CHAPTER 1: THE BEST OF TIMES

Soundtrack: The Jam – "When You're Young"

"RISE AND SHINE, citizens of La Jolla! It's going to be another beautiful sunny day!"

Tommy Daniels snaps awake and turns off the alarm on his clock radio. He's not the kind of person who wears his emotions on his sleeve, but on this particular Thursday morning in August, Tommy has a smile etched onto his face.

Why the good mood? Tommy's life has been building up to this week for nearly eighteen years. He's days away from having sex for the first time, choosing classes for his first semester of college, and having enough money to afford his dream vehicle: the ultimate symbol of Mod culture, the Vespa.

Filled with positive energy, Tommy reaches over and grabs one of his prized possessions: an old issue of *Melody Maker* from 1980 featuring two generations of Mod musical icons, Pete Townshend and Paul Weller, on the cover. He picked it up at a garage sale a couple years ago for a dollar. He's read it more times than he can count and it is totally worn out, looking like it's been chewed up by the garbage disposal. He flips through a few pages to get his brain going.

One glance at Tommy's room and there is no doubt that he is obsessed with Mod culture. The place is a fuckin' shrine to *Quadrophenia*, the Who, the Jam, and—of course—the coolest vehicle in the world, the Vespa. He tries his best to fit the Mod aesthetic: medium-length, shaggy brown hair that falls onto his forehead and a fitted suit that he wears when he goes out on the town. Even his naturally thin, 5-foot-9-inch frame seems ideally Mod.

Still, seeing as this is August 1985, Tommy doesn't exactly fit in with the times. No one around him shares his tastes. La Jolla, the Southern California beach town he lives in, is suburban, upper class, and bland. His family's house is cookie cutter and without color. Mod culture speaks to Tommy because it is so different: urban, edgy, streamlined, cool.

After spending the requisite amount of time affirming the merits of being Mod, Tommy takes thirty minutes to read through a chapter in a film textbook. Tommy tears through multiple books each week and has an uncanny knack of absorbing most everything he reads. He is smart. Really smart. He aced all his AP classes and his scores on the SATs were in the top percentile. He's less than a month away from starting at a great college and, though they aren't rich, his family has managed to put away enough to pay for his first year.

He wants to study film and dreams of becoming a big-time director. He's a huge fan of George Lucas, but not just because of *Star Wars*. Tommy has seen *American Graffiti* ten times and dreams of making a similar coming-of-age movie about a Mod-obsessed teenager living in a dull Southern California town. Come to think of it, the story might be a *tad* autobiographical.

Tommy's attention starts to drift. Being a seventeen-year-old boy, there's one thing that's never far from his mind: girls. And Tommy's got a good one. Stephanie Oshiro is cute, smart, and ready to go all the way with Tommy, as soon as she turns eighteen this Saturday and before she leaves to become a freshman at USC. No wonder Tommy is in a good mood, right? Stephanie's dad runs the local operations for some Japanese electronics conglomerate, so suffice it to say, the Oshiros are filthy rich. For fuck's sake, their butler has a personal assistant.

Tommy glances over at his bedroom door and sees something unexpected: a box wrapped with expensive-looking paper and a bow. He leaps over and tears it open. Inside, he finds the coolest gift he's ever gotten: a Walkman. Inside it is a tape with the label "Tommy's Mod Mixtape."

It is accompanied by a note: "Dearest Tommy, you've talked about how great these songs are so many times. So, I had the audio guy at my dad's company put this tape together. I even had him put on that song by the Kinks that you played the first time we kissed! There are two copies of the mixtape: one for you and one for me. Maybe we can play it on Saturday night? Love, Stephanie."

On the back of the note is a list of all the bands on the tape. Tommy's mouth drops as he sees the names: the Jam, the Who, Chardon Square, Squire, the Action, the Kinks, Manual Scan, the Rain Parade, the Untouchables, Agent Orange, Small Faces, the Plimsouls, the Chords, the Question, the Three O'Clock, Secret Affair, and General Public. It's like the soundtrack of his entire life!

Tommy puts on his headphones and plays the first song. He dances around as the Jam's "When You're Young" blasts in his ears.

Afterward, he sprints over to the phone and dials with overwhelming teenage (i.e., horny) excitement. Stephanie picks up.

"You're amazing!" Tommy exclaims. "The Walkman is totally cool! And the mixtape is rad beyond words!"

Stephanie giggles.

"My dad brought home a couple Walkmans and I thought you'd like one. I've never really listened that much to the music you're obsessed with, but I promise I will now."

"Steph, you're the best! You're going to love these songs."

"I hope so. So . . . what are we doing Friday after dinner?" Stephanie asks. "It's your turn to plan something."

"Let's grab some coffee and then walk down to the beach."

"That sounds incredible," Stephanie responds, clearly cheerful at the thought of spending time with her boyfriend.

The call goes on for another few minutes, but not much is said. Mainly, they just sigh like some silly, love-struck teenagers . . . which is exactly what they are.

Hanging up the phone, Tommy puts his headphones back on briefly, but then glimpses the time on the clock radio. He's running late for work! He gets dressed in a hurry and rushes out the door.

Tommy may not come from a wealthy family, but he works hard. He slogs five days a week for Jack's Drugs as a delivery boy. He drives a truck and delivers pills and contraceptives to the rich and entitled of La Jolla. Some of the people are pretty nice, giving him generous tips and saying things like "thank you" and "have a nice day." A lot of them are total assholes, grabbing their pills and slamming the door, complaining that he's late, or yelling at him for messing something up, like he's the pharmacist.

Tommy drives to his first few deliveries, eagerly anticipating some of the rich forty- and fifty-something housewives on his route. They often come to the door in revealing workout clothes, robes that are half-open, or towels that are seconds away from slipping off. Tommy has gotten more peeks at middle-aged breasts than probably anyone outside of the porn industry. Even better, some of these women gently flirt with him. Nothing serious, but enough to get Tommy to fantasize about what it would be like to have sex with an older woman. He imagines that, with their experience, it would be amazing.

Around noon, Tommy delivers pills to his favorite customer, Dr. Harvey, a kindly old, very eccentric, and incredibly rich children's author. Dr. Harvey was a member of the Beat Generation back in the 1950s and he continues to be a nonconformist in many ways.

Tommy opens the unlocked front door and gazes around the living room of Dr. Harvey's strange house. He has been there numerous times, but Tommy can't get over how peculiar it is. There are bright colors everywhere, weird psychedelic images drawn directly on the walls, and sculptures that are the definition of zany. He has a room in his house devoted entirely to his strange assortment of hats! Tommy loves Dr. Harvey and his house precisely because they are so out of place in La Jolla.

Tommy enters Dr. Harvey's office, where the author sits on a bean bag chair.

"Come on in, Mr. Daniels! It looks like the world is treating you nicely. How can it not be? You're a young man filled with visions and desires, and you have it in yourself to make them happen!"

Tommy laughs at Dr. Harvey's overblown greeting. He stares at the renowned children's author, taking in his strange persona. At first glance, he resembles Santa Claus: big white beard, fat gut, and jolly laugh. His off-the-wall attitude is reflected in his sweater, with its bright colors, bizarre patterns, and strange drawings. Likewise, he sports one of his many multihued and oddly shaped hats: a purple beret with a small sculpture of a cat riding on top of a dog, who is riding on top of an elephant, who is balanced on top of an Asian man. Dr. Harvey's sense of style is completed by his thick, horn-rimmed glasses, which seem entirely too large for his face.

Tommy plops down on a ridiculously giant polka dot armchair, his regular spot. Tommy visits so frequently because Dr. Harvey is a pillhead, totally addicted to pain killers. Tommy typically sits and shoots the breeze, as Dr. Harvey pops his pills. Despite the age difference, it seems to Tommy that they have a real connection and that the offbeat author likes Tommy just as much as Tommy likes him. Dr. Harvey listens to Tommy talk about everything: his girlfriend, schoolwork, fantasies of sleeping with the hot older women on his route. Of course, their discussions inevitably turn to Tommy's favorite topic: Vespas. Dr. Harvey takes copious notes during all their conversations.

On this visit, Tommy takes out a trade magazine from his back pocket, opens it to a specific page, and hands it to Dr. Harvey.

"Dr. Harvey, I found this incredible Vespa!"

He waits a few moments as Dr. Harvey stares at the image of the scooter in the magazine.

"It's twenty-five hundred dollars," Tommy blurts out. "I don't have enough money, but if I can get the guy to lower the price a bit, I should be able to get it!"

Dr. Harvey makes a few notes on his yellow pad.

"That's fabulously, ferociously fantastic, Tommy! You've always made your dreams your guide, now it's time to get yourself a ride!"

Tommy chuckles. He loves it when Dr. Harvey randomly rhymes and uses alliteration. It sometimes sounds like he's reading from one of his books.

Dr. Harvey smokes pot and takes more pills while Tommy goes on and on about this new Vespa: its beautiful paint job, how it'll handle, the way he'll look riding it, and so on.

After a while, Tommy notices that Dr. Harvey is passed out. He's not sure how much Dr. Harvey actually heard about the scooter he plans to buy.

On his way out, Tommy whispers, "Have a nice nap, Dr. Harvey."

CHAPTER 2: VESPA DREAMIN'

Soundtrack: The Who – "I Can't Explain"

THOUGH EVERYTHING SEEMS to be going well, Tommy's life is far from perfect. His parents can't afford to live in a place like La Jolla. They just do so because Frank, Tommy's dad, thinks it's good for the family to live with rich people. His dad always envied the people in La Jolla growing up and moved there soon after Tommy was born, even though it made no economic sense.

So, the Daniels family lives beyond their means. They rent their home, which is unheard of in La Jolla unless you are renting short-term while your real house undergoes renovations. All their friends and neighbors believe the Daniels family owns their very fabulous house. Some of the residents on their street have commented that it's weird that the Daniels family only owns one, late model car (a station wagon, no less). But otherwise, there are few rumblings that the Daniels family is not among the blessed rich of La Jolla.

Tommy's parents love each other, but constantly fight because they never have any money. Rebecca, Tommy's mom, is only forty, but looks a good ten years older because of the constant stress.

When Tommy asks his mom about his tuition payment on Thursday morning—he starts college in just about a month—she awkwardly changes the subject.

"Hey, honey, have you heard about all those robberies at the Swiftee Marts? You better be careful!"

She drones on about the spate of robberies for what feels like five minutes. Tommy ignores her, putting on headphones and pressing play on his Walkman. Who the fuck cares about Swiftee Marts?

Thursday evening. Tommy gets home from work with a stack of cash in his hand. He rushes to his room and takes out a tin filled with money from his closet. He adds his cash to the pile and counts it. He has $2,311.

He grabs his trade magazine, which is opened to the page with his dream Vespa: a white 1963 GS. It's being sold by Gordy's Scooter Boutique, located in South Beach, Florida. It's listed for $2,500, but Tommy thinks he can get the seller to come down on the price. Given the time difference in Florida, Tommy knows he can't call until the morning. He falls asleep with the magazine on his chest.

All night, he dreams of riding the Vespa on the open road with Stephanie on the back. They are young, happy, and horny. So, life is good. Given his love of the movies, Tommy's dreams always have a cinematic quality to them. As the song "I Can't Explain" by the Who plays, Tommy pulls the Vespa over on the side of a deserted road. He spreads out a blanket. He and Stephanie are suddenly naked. They have the kind of sex you see in the movies: clean, romantic, epic. Clearly, watching HBO at his friend's house last week had a big effect on him.

In the morning, Tommy snaps awake. He wipes away the drool and grabs the phone and dials. He reaches Gordy, an old, grumpy-sounding Englishman. Tommy explains where he lives and asks about the Vespa.

Gordy blurts, "It's three thousand dollars, mate!"

Tommy is flummoxed.

"But it's only twenty-five hundred dollars in your ad!"

"Shit. Umm, okay. I'll take twenty-five hundred then!"

"I can offer you two thousand."

"Bloody hell. That's barely enough to wipe my ass after a big meal."

"Sir, I can offer you twenty-one hundred."

"Hold on a second."

Gordy puts the phone down and vomits for about thirty seconds. Tommy is grossed out.

"Are you okay, sir?"

"Yeah, I'm fine. Just had a good time last night with some old mates. You seem like a nice bloke, calling me 'sir' all the time like I've been knighted by the bloody queen. How about this? I'll take twenty-three hundred.

"Deal!"

"And it'll be five hundred to ship it to you in La Jolla."

"Five hundred dollars? I don't have money for that!"

"Blimey, take it down a few decibels. Listen up. I have a big shipment going to a dealership in Santa Barbara in a week. Your Vespa can hitch a ride for free, if you're willing to go pick it up."

Tommy dances around his room, as Gordy breaks down all the details. Tommy has to wire $300 and then the Vespa will arrive at the dealership in Santa Barbara in a little more than a week.

Once he gets his scooter, Tommy will be able to stop bumming rides from his friends, parents, and, worst of all, Stephanie. Every time he has to ask Stephanie to drive him somewhere, he feels like his dick gets just a little smaller. And no one as hot as Stephanie is going to have sex with a small-dicked guy with no wheels.

CHAPTER 3: CRUMBLING FOUNDATION

 *Soundtrack: Chardon Square – "65 Film Show"*

AFTER WIRING THE $300 to Gordy, Tommy cheerfully goes to work. He delivers drugs to various hot older women. Mrs. Zenda, a forty-year-old mother of three, may be the hottest on this day. She walks to the door in a skimpy bathing suit.

"Hey, sweetie, good timing. I was just about to go for a swim."

Tommy keeps his eyes up, trying really hard not to seem like a pervert.

"Here is your prescription."

"You seem like you're in a good mood!"

Tommy grins widely.

"I am! I got some good news."

"Excellent, honey. I could use some of that positive energy. You want to join me for a swim?"

Visions of Mrs. Robinson dance around in Tommy's head. Is she really coming onto me? he wonders. Of course, most of these ladies flirt with Tommy just to get a kick. They would probably call the police if he put a hand anywhere on their bodies. It doesn't matter anyway, because Tommy has only two things on his mind: the Vespa and Stephanie.

"No, thanks, Mrs. Zenda. I have some deliveries to make."

He goes to Dr. Harvey's house next. As usual, the front door is unlocked, so Tommy lets himself in. He finds Dr. Harvey on the couch, not moving and wearing a large hat covered with porcupine quills. Tommy pokes him a couple times.

"Hey, man. I have your pills."

When Dr. Harvey still doesn't move, Tommy starts to worry. He listens to his chest and doesn't hear a heartbeat.

"Crap!"

Tommy doesn't know CPR, but he has seen a shit ton of movies, so he thinks he's got the basics. He breathes into Dr. Harvey's mouth. Nothing happens. He pushes down on Dr. Harvey's chest really hard a couple of times, using all the force his lanky frame can muster.

Dr. Harvey leaps up.

"For fuck's sake! Are you trying to kill me? Or was that some kind of messed up sexual thing the kids are doing these days?"

Tommy sits back, relieved more than anything.

"I thought you were dead, man."

Dr. Harvey laughs and slaps Tommy on the back playfully.

"No such luck!"

Dr. Harvey grabs the bag from Tommy, leans back on the couch, and swallows a bunch of pills. Tommy sits next to him and tells him about all the good things that are about to come into his life, namely the Vespa and sex with his hot girlfriend.

Dr. Harvey takes plenty of notes, particularly when Tommy gives details about the Vespa.

He chimes in, "A cool ride and a hot chick. What more could you want?"

Eventually, Tommy finishes talking about his Vespa and Dr. Harvey pays him with cash, as usual.

After dropping off the delivery truck at the pharmacy, Tommy heads to the Swiftee Mart to grab a soda. He tries to push the front door open, but it won't budge. He stumbles backwards clumsily, leading some nearby skaters to laugh.

One of them shouts, "Learn to read, dude!"

Tommy looks in the window and sees a handwritten sign: "Big waves, gone surfing." He shakes his head. That's what happens when a store is run by a bunch of skinhead surfers.

Friday night at the Daniels house. Tommy paces back and forth by the front door, playing Chardon Square's "65 Film Show" on his Walkman while waiting for Stephanie to come over for dinner. Stephanie has met his parents several times, but she has never come over for dinner before. On their dates, Stephanie usually picks Tommy up in the driveway and they head out to do something or go over to her fancy house.

But when Tommy's mom ran into Stephanie a couple days ago, she insisted that Stephanie come over for dinner on Friday. Tommy doesn't really understand why. The Daniels family rarely has dinner in the traditional sense. Tommy's mom or dad usually buys or (once in a while) makes dinner, and the family members just grab some whenever they have time. They plop down and eat in front of the TV or in their own bedrooms. Tommy thinks his mom is just trying to show Stephanie that they're fancier than they really are. Such bullshit.

When Stephanie arrives at 8:30 p.m., she and Tommy both exude nervousness. They hug awkwardly and head into the dining room, which is almost never used for dining purposes, operating as a makeshift office to store and pay bills.

As soon as Tommy sees his parents, he knows the dinner is a huge mistake. Tommy's dad is sitting at the table with a "Pay Rent or Quit" notice. He looks beyond miserable. Next to him, Tommy's mom is crying.

"Frank, what are we going to do? We barely have a dollar in the bank. Where would we move?"

Tommy's dad puts his hands through his hair, sweat dripping down all over his face and neck.

"I have a follow-up job interview tomorrow. Maybe they'll hire me."

Tommy looks over and sees the expression on Stephanie's face: a mixture of horror and pity. She had clearly never suspected that the Daniels family had money problems or that they rented their house, mainly because Tommy had always done his darnedest to keep her in the dark. Yes, Tommy never had any money and didn't own a car, but Stephanie had assumed it was because his parents were hard asses, wanting him to work for everything on his own. Tommy had done nothing to dissuade this notion.

Tommy feels an overwhelming sense of shame. Stephanie obviously wants to get out of there, but is too polite to act like she witnessed anything unpleasant.

"Mr. and Mrs. Daniels. Such a pleasure to see you both! It's a thrill to be invited over for dinner. My dad asked me to bring over this bottle of wine as a thank you."

Finally realizing that Tommy and Stephanie are in the room, Tommy's parents both seem embarrassed. Stephanie hands Mrs.

Daniels the bottle of wine. Tommy's mom looks panic-stricken, obviously having forgotten that Stephanie was coming over . . . or that she was supposed to make dinner.

An hour later, the Daniels family and Stephanie are seated around the dining room table eating pizza delivered from Sabato's, a local pizza joint. Tommy is sick of pizza. It is by far the most common dish served at the Daniels house. Everyone eats pretty silently, except for some silly small talk.

Tommy's parents take the dirty plates into the kitchen at the end of the meal. Tommy and Stephanie stay in the dining room, awkwardly sipping soda for a few minutes. When they take their glasses into the kitchen, they see Mr. and Mrs. Daniels standing in the backyard.

As he puts his hands on his wife's shoulders, Tommy's dad says, "We'll get through this. We've made it through worse."

Tommy's mom wipes away her tears and replies, "It's a good thing we never unpacked those old boxes in the garage."

They laugh through their pain.

Stephanie gazes at Mrs. Daniels and seems to study her face, with its prominent lines caused by years of stress. She then turns to the mirror in the kitchen and looks at her own face, so fresh and wrinkle-free. Stephanie's mouth opens in distinct horror, but she quickly puts on a smile when she notices Tommy staring at her.

Leaving Tommy's parents behind, Stephanie and Tommy head to Pannikin Coffee & Tea, the local hangout for cool kids. Stephanie is totally silent as she drives.

Tommy smiles and asks, "What's wrong, Steph?"

Seeming to be in a trance, Stephanie responds, "Nothing. Just a little nervous about Saturday."

Tommy thinks he understands. Who wouldn't be nervous about their first time having sex? Heaven knows, Tommy is nervous as hell. But he's also tired of jacking off three times a day. At this point, he's developing wrist problems.

At Pannikin, Tommy and Stephanie order a pastry and sit on the patio. A brand new Porsche screeches to a halt directly in front of them. Out steps David W. Tush, the school jock. He's a pretentious, rich-kid asshole. Seriously, if he ever makes himself business cards, that's pretty much what he would have to list under his name, since it describes him to a T.

David struts to Stephanie, jutting out his muscular chest. He clearly has a thing for Stephanie and keeps pursuing her, despite the fact that she's been with Tommy for more than six months. Tommy fuckin' hates his guts.

David tilts his head seductively (or at least he thinks it's seductive).

"Hey Steph. See my new ride?"

Stephanie smiles and responds, "Yeah, it's pretty nice. My uncle has the same car."

Tommy gets uncomfortable whenever the rich in La Jolla discuss their expensive things, mainly because it just reminds him how hard-up his family is for money and how everyone here takes for granted that everyone has money.

David continues to pretend that Tommy isn't there.

"So, Stephanie, are you going to the ball on Saturday?"

There's a fucking socialite ball every weekend in La Jolla.

Before Stephanie can answer, Tommy sticks his super skinny chest out and faces the much taller David.

"No, David, we're going to Club Zu on Saturday. Anyway, Stephanie doesn't like lame socialite events."

The truth is Stephanie doesn't mind them, but Tommy hates the superficiality and falseness of everyone at these events.

David grins and condescendingly pats Tommy on the shoulder before walking away. Tommy and Stephanie sit back down. The waitress brings their check: $10. Tommy knows he barely has a dollar to spare if he is going to make it to Santa Barbara to buy his Vespa next week. So, he slides the check over to Stephanie and smiles sheepishly.

"Baby, can you take care of this? I'm strapped and need all my cash for my Vespa."

Stephanie nods sadly and takes out some cash.

Tommy wants to go down to the beach to take "a walk" (i.e., make out at length), but Stephanie claims she's too tired. So, she takes Tommy home.

She pulls into his driveway really slowly, as if she's stretching out the moments and recording them in her memory. When she turns the car off, Tommy leans over to kiss his girlfriend, but she blocks him with her hand.

"Please, stop."

Confused, Tommy asks, "What's wrong?"

"Tommy, the truth is I've been thinking about things and I don't want to end up like your mom."

"My mom? What does she have to do with anything?"

"I saw her tonight and she was so exhausted and looked so sad . . . all because of your family's money problems."

Stephanie tenderly puts her hands on Tommy's face.

"I love you, but if we sleep together tomorrow, I feel like I'm going to be trapped with you. I mean, I don't know if I'd be able to leave you after we go through with that. And I want to have a better life than the one your mother has."

Tommy gets upset.

"But it won't be like that! I'll find a way to take care of us both. I'll make movies and make lots of money!"

Crying, Stephanie gazes into Tommy's eyes.

"You are such a dreamer. That's all you do. But you don't have enough money to buy me a pastry at a café. And you don't even have a car to pick me up and take me out."

"But I'm getting my Vespa soon! I should have it in a week!"

"Stop dreaming about getting a silly scooter! Your family doesn't have enough to pay their rent!"

Tommy tries to take Stephanie's hand.

"I love you, Stephanie."

Stephanie pulls away.

"It's over, Tommy."

Stephanie turns the car on and puts it in reverse, waiting for Tommy to get out. In shock, he exits. He watches as she speeds away down the street.

Fuckin' teenage heartbreak.

CHAPTER 4: DOWNWARD SPIRAL

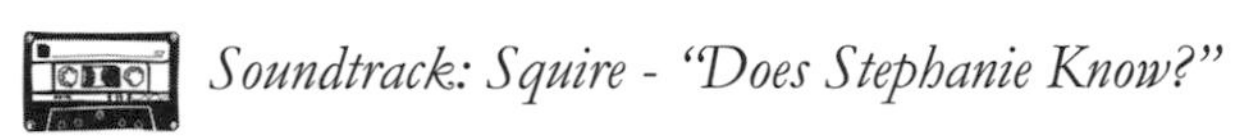
Soundtrack: Squire - "Does Stephanie Know?"

IT'S MIDNIGHT WHEN Tommy walks through the front door of the Daniels house. Most of the lights are off, so Tommy stands crying in the darkness for a few minutes. Then, he peeks into his parents' room and sees his mom sleeping like a log. She's a stress case, particularly with all their financial issues, so she takes some pretty strong tranquilizers every night. We're talking shit that could knock out an overweight horse.

Tommy notices a lamp is on inside the living room. He wanders in to find his dad sitting alone, staring down at the family's bills. His dad looks up at Tommy with bloodshot eyes. He's been crying. Evidently, it's been an emotional night for both Daniels men.

Tommy somberly stares at his dad.

"What are you doing up, Dad?"

His dad averts his eyes from Tommy.

"Searching for a way out of this. I don't know what to do, Son. We don't have any money. This is the first time your mom and I have been out of work at the same time."

Tommy feels pangs of guilt for all the money the family has set aside for his first year of college.

"Dad, this is my fault. I know you already paid for my first semester of college, but the second semester bill won't come until the start of next year. Why don't you use some of that money to pay rent and some of the bills?"

Tommy's dad's face crumbles. He runs his hands through his thinning hair.

"Son, I have to confess something. We already spent that money."

Flabbergasted that his dad didn't tell him this earlier, Tommy does his best not to make the situation worse.

"It's okay, Dad. I'm sure you needed it. I'll figure something out for the second semester. Thanks for paying for my first semester. It means a lot."

Tommy's dad takes a deep breath, appearing even more grief-stricken.

"Tommy, we had to use that money too."

Tommy loses his cool.

"What the fuck, Dad! You know I start school in under a month! I've probably already missed some payment deadlines! Why didn't you say something sooner?"

"We talked to your school. We broke down your first semester tuition payments into four installments. We paid the first installment. The second installment won't be due for more than two months. We'll figure out a way to pay it."

"Yeah, right! You've done such a great job of figuring out how to pay our rent."

Tommy storms out and heads to his bedroom. He takes out the metal chest he keeps in his closet. He pulls out a few joints, some booze, and a Playboy magazine featuring a girl who looks like Stephanie with much bigger tits. He contemplates getting high and drunk and masturbating for a while (the trifecta of teenage solo pleasures).

But, instead, he takes out the tin that contains all his money for the Vespa. He counts $2000 and puts the remaining few dollars into his pocket. Tommy sighs. He knows he can't use the cash for a Vespa anymore, not with his family in such dire straits. The question is, should he use the money to help his dad or to pay for his college? The pathetic look on his dad's face moments earlier and Tommy's deep love for his parents make the answer obvious.

Tommy marches up to his dad and holds out the wad of cash. His dad slowly looks up at Tommy. Shame washes over his face. Tommy knows what his dad is probably thinking: He should be able to take care of his family without resorting to help from his teenage son. Nevertheless, Tommy's dad sets his pride aside and takes the money. He takes a piece of paper and writes Tommy an IOU.

Tommy walks away, feeling deeply sad. He remembers a time when his dad seemed like the most powerful man in the world. Now he's just another guy desperately scrounging around for a few bucks.

With only $11 left, Tommy goes into his room where he pulls out an envelope filled with IOUs from his dad. He tosses this one in.

He puts on his headphones and presses play on his Walkman. The song? Squire's "Does Stephanie Know?" Pretty damn great timing, right?

Tommy falls into bed and stares at the ceiling. At least things can't get any worse.

The next morning, Tommy quickly learns something: Things can always get worse. At 6:30 a.m., he wakes up feeling like garbage: congested, dizzy, coughing up a storm. He barely slept all night. In the harsh light of day, he replays the events of the previous night. How could things have gone so wrong so fast? He has no money for his Vespa, owes a shitload of money for his first semester of college, and got dumped by his girlfriend. Yeah, that's a lot of bad stuff for one night.

He mourns the fact that this was supposed to be the night that he and Stephanie finally went all the way. He picks up the phone and dials her.

Stephanie groggily answers her phone, "Hello?"

Having pumped himself up, Tommy blurts, "Stephanie, it's me. I love you. Please, let's work it out!"

Dashing any hopes of reconciliation, she states in a matter-of-fact tone, "Tommy, it's over. Move on. Have a nice life."

Before she puts the phone back on the receiver, Tommy hears a male voice in the background ask, "Who's on the phone, baby?"

Tommy's mouth drops. He would recognize David W. Tush's voice anywhere.

Tommy listens as Stephanie responds, "Wrong number," before hanging up.

Tommy slams the phone down and screams, "Mother fucker!"

He fumes. Last night, he had a girlfriend. She's gone now and, what's worse, she's fucking that piece of shit, David!

It's 7:15 a.m. Tommy and his dad share a tense breakfast at the kitchen table. Tommy, pissed for so many reasons, glowers at his father in between inhaling his corn flakes. His dad still clearly feels embarrassed by the whole thing.

"I'm sorry, Tommy. I'll make it up to you, somehow."

Tommy is in no mood for apologies.

"Yeah, right. I wish you'd get your shit together, Dad. I'm going to end up supporting Mom someday!"

Indignant, his dad responds, "Listen, Tommy, I know you're upset, but everything I've done has been for you. Do you know how lucky you are that you get to live in La Jolla? I grew up in Riverside, goddamnit!"

Tommy shakes his head.

"Yeah, I'm lucky to live with all the rich assholes here."

The two Daniels men sit in silence for about a minute, both seething with righteous anger. Tommy finally stands up.

"I need to use the car to run some errands."

His dad nods.

"Okay, but I need it back this afternoon to go to my interview."

It's 8 a.m. and Tommy is parked outside of Stephanie's house in his parents' station wagon. He has his headphones on, listening to the mixtape Stephanie made for what feels like the thousandth time since she broke up with him.

He knows Stephanie's parents are out of town (that's why this was supposed to be their big sex weekend), so he ponders knocking on the door and making a scene. But he can't bring himself to get out of the car. All he can do is sit there and sneer at David W. Tush's brand new fuckin' Porsche sitting in the Oshiro driveway.

A million thoughts rush in and out of Tommy's head until only one remains: revenge. Tommy turns on the car. He drives past the driveway, then stops and puts the car in reverse. He hits the gas, backing his parents' land yacht right into David's glorious Porsche. The crunching sound is music to Tommy's ears. David's car alarm goes off. Tommy puts the station wagon into drive and screeches away.

He parks on the next street, then runs back and hides in the bushes to see how things unfold. He sees Stephanie looking out of her bedroom window. A minute later, David exits wearing only his underwear.

David makes it to the driveway and sees his car. Horror. Pain. If you didn't know better, you'd think he just got kicked in the balls. Wearing nothing but tighty-whities and screaming to the heavens, David makes quite the spectacle. He turns to Stephanie, as she peeks out from behind the front door wearing only a sheet.

"Did you see anything? Maybe a license plate?"

Stephanie nervously responds, "Me? No, nothing. I heard a car screeching but when I looked, it was already gone."

Watching her twitch, Tommy guesses she saw him drive off and is covering for him for some reason.

David and Stephanie go inside and come back out two minutes later. She's fully dressed, but he is still missing a shirt. Stephanie turns to David.

"David, I hope you realize this was a one-time thing."

David turns red with anger.

"What the fuck, babe? My car just got smashed to hell and you're breaking up with me!"

"We aren't breaking up! We were never dating. I just wanted to have sex before leaving for college. I did it with you because I don't like you very much. I don't want to leave La Jolla with any strings attached."

She tosses David his shirt.

"You can go now."

David turns to Stephanie.

"You have no idea what you're missing, babe!"

Stephanie looks down at David's crotch area.

"Not much."

She slams the door on his shocked face. David gets into his damaged car and drives away, his mangled rear bumper scraping the asphalt.

A few seconds later, Tommy can hear Stephanie just inside the front door, bawling uncontrollably. Too angry to feel sympathy, he walks away.

CHAPTER 5: THE DOCTOR DELIVERS

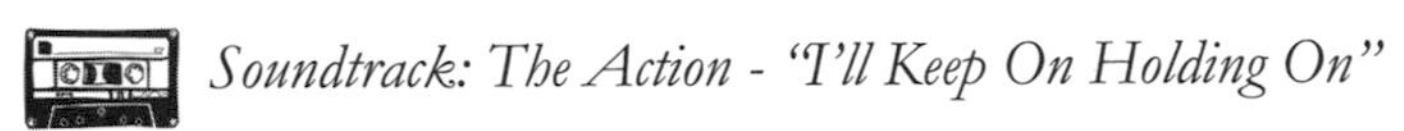

Soundtrack: The Action - "I'll Keep On Holding On"

TOMMY LEAVES THE station wagon in his family's driveway. His parents probably won't notice the large new dent, since the car already had a ton of them from countless little fender-benders over the years. From the back, the station wagon looks like it's been through a war.

Tommy hikes over to the pharmacy, grabs the keys to his delivery truck, and gets to work. Depressed, losing hope that he can ever get his Vespa or pay for college, Tommy robotically makes his deliveries. He is too downcast to play along or even get turned on when the hot housewives flirt with him. The only thing he looks forward to is his regular delivery to Dr. Harvey.

Tommy enters Dr. Harvey's house and sees the writer sprawled on the couch, smiling. His hat today is definitely not subdued: a green beret covered with a multihued assortment of dried daisies. Tommy hands him his pills and Dr. Harvey immediately pops a few.

Sitting on a bean bag chair, Tommy recounts the events of the past day. He complains about not having the money for his Vespa or college, rails against Stephanie, insults David, and celebrates his destruction of the Porsche.

Dr. Harvey shakes his head.

"She tells you she loves you and fucks another guy? That's messed up, man."

Dr. Harvey smirks.

"I don't normally condone the destruction of private property, but that Tushy guy had it coming."

Tommy laughs for a second at his nemesis being called "Tushy" (it sums up how much of an ass David is). But then he returns to feeling sorry for himself.

"Dr. Harvey, I was so fuckin' close to getting my Vespa. I even paid the deposit! I don't how I'm going to get that back. I had the rest of the money and then, poof, it was gone. Now, I don't have shit."

Dr. Harvey abruptly gets up and goes down the hallway to another room. It's not entirely unexpected. During their meetings, Dr. Harvey frequently disappears for a few minutes and returns wearing a new, even stranger hat.

To Tommy's surprise, this time Dr. Harvey returns wearing the exact same hat, though he does have a noticeable bulge in the front right pocket of his pants. For a moment, Tommy wonders if Dr. Harvey has a ridiculously large penis. But then he realizes the inscrutable shape in his pants doesn't quite match that of the male appendage.

Dr. Harvey takes some pills, while Tommy complains some more. After a few minutes, Dr. Harvey appears extra spacey and sleepy. Tommy knows that's his cue to leave and moves to the door.

"Hey, man, catch!" Dr. Harvey yells out.

He takes an envelope out of his pocket and tosses it to Tommy, who fumbles it for a second.

"What is this?" Tommy asks.

He opens the envelope and sees a wad of cash. He counts $2,000! Tommy can't believe it. He wants the money, of course, but he doesn't want Dr. Harvey's charity. He likes that they are truly friends. Taking money from him might mess that up.

"This is incredible, Dr. Harvey, but I can't take the money. I wouldn't feel right about it."

Dr. Harvey laughs.

"This isn't charity, kid. You've earned it. I'm paying you for the work you helped me with."

Tommy shakes his head.

"The pharmacy pays me and you tip me pretty well every time I come by. We're good."

"No, no, no."

Dr. Harvey strokes his Santa Claus beard.

"I've written a new children's book and our conversations were the inspiration."

"Our conversations? What's the book about?"

Dr. Harvey's eyes light up.

"It's called *Victor the Vespa*, man! It's about a Vespa who doesn't fit in with the trucks, cars, and motorcycles in his crappy town. The publishers love it. I'm going to make a shitload of money on this one!"

Tommy stills looks confused.

"So . . . this money is for inspiring your book?"

"Yes, that's part of it. I just want one other thing. I want you to keep coming by even after you start college. At least a couple times a month, stop on by and shoot the breeze. I think there may be more book ideas I can get from our chats."

Tommy gets awkwardly emotional, fighting back tears.

"You don't know how much this means to me, Dr. Harvey."

Though Tommy wants to use the money for his Vespa more than anything, he decides to be more responsible.

"I guess I should use this money for college. That would be the smart thing to do."

Dr. Harvey bounces up from the couch.

"Smart thing? Man, you know why I like you so much?"

He puts his hands on Tommy's shoulders.

"You're an honest to goodness dreamer. The smart thing for you would have been to try to fit in with all the rich pieces of shit in this town. But you march to the beat of your own drum. What has been your dream for most of your life, man?"

Tommy smiles.

"To own a Vespa."

Dr. Harvey stares seriously into Tommy's eyes.

"You've got to make your dreams come true now. Not later. I wrote a book about a Vespa after hearing you talk about Vespas for a couple years. It's only right that you use the money to buy a Vespa. In fact, if you want to use it for anything else, I'm taking the money back."

Tommy is convinced. He hugs Dr. Harvey and heads home with a renewed zest for life.

He calls Gordy in Florida and learns that his Vespa will be delivered in one week to a place called Val's Vespa Emporium in Santa Barbara. He can't wait.

For Tommy Daniels, life is definitely getting good again.

PART 2: THE SCOOTER CHRONICLES

CHAPTER 6: DICK

 *Soundtrack: The Kinks - "David Watts"*

A WEEK HAS passed. It's the big day and Tommy couldn't be more pumped. He finishes up his deliveries way ahead of schedule and makes it to the bus station at 2:30 p.m., a full thirty minutes early. He's dressed in tight Levi's jeans, a Fred Perry shirt, desert boots, and a parka. Classic casual Mod.

Tommy listens to his mixtape as he waits for the bus. Having some free time, he thinks about how important getting a Vespa is to him. He knows it seems a bit ridiculous, but he believes that once he gets his Vespa, everything in his life will start coming together. It'll be a domino effect.

About twenty feet from Tommy, a fat cop with a shockingly thick mustache hassles some surfers, who are waiting for a bus with their surfboards in hand.

"Are you kids high on pot? Your eyes look bloodshot. Have you been smoking up some doobies? Our town doesn't put up with that stuff."

The surfers giggle a little, most likely because they are indeed a bit high. This only riles the cop more.

"What do you think you're laughing at, potheads? What's with your hair, anyway? I think all that bleach has melted your damn brains!"

What an asshole. Tommy shakes his head.

Tommy's bus pulls up and he shakes with anticipation. In about four hours, he'll be in Santa Barbara to get his Vespa! On his headphones, he hears the Kinks's "David Watts," the song playing when he kissed Stephanie for the first time.

Tommy thinks back to that night. It was raining, so he and Stephanie were huddled up listening to music on her living room couch. He was insanely nervous. After thinking about it for what felt like an eternity, he finally leaned in and pressed his lips against hers.

Listening to the song's lyrics about longing to have the charmed life of David Watts, Tommy suddenly starts thinking about another David . . . David W. Tush. He broods over David's perpetually smug face and rich lifestyle and how Stephanie chose to lose her virginity to that total jerk!

Filled with fury, Tommy rips the mixtape out of the Walkman and stares at it for a moment. Then, he throws it to the ground and smashes it to smithereens with his foot.

He exhales. With the mixtape gone, he feels that he has finally left Stephanie behind.

What he's not leaving behind is the Mod music that he loves. The songs are forever burned into Tommy's mind and will continue to play in his head everywhere he goes. Anyway, he will listen to his favorite songs again when he returns home to his cassette and LP collection.

He moves toward the bus.

"Stop right there, punk!" the cop shouts out.

Great, he thinks he's frickin' Dirty Harry. Tommy turns as the cop approaches him.

"Damn it, kid, are you an idiot? You can't litter like that. Not in La Jolla!"

The cop points to the name tag on his uniform.

"I'm Officer Richard and I don't put up with shenanigans like that in my town."

Tommy ponders running into the bus and telling the driver to hit the gas. Upon second thought, he realizes that might work in the movies, but probably not in La Jolla.

The cop grabs Tommy's Walkman and studies it.

"Another spoiled rich kid, eh?"

"Officer Richard, I'm sorry," Tommy pleads. "I made a mistake. Please let me go. This is the last bus I can take to Santa Barbara today, and I really need to get there."

Unsympathetic, the officer responds, "Don't do the crime if you can't do the time! Well, actually, you're not going to jail, but you *are* getting a ticket."

Tommy watches in horror as his bus leaves for Santa Barbara. Waiting as the asshole cop writes him his ticket, Tommy feels himself getting angrier and angrier, until he can't hold it in any longer.

"Officer Richard? They should really call you Officer Dick."

Having probably heard that appropriate nickname before, Officer Dick briefly grins at Tommy and hands him his ticket.

"Listen, kid, you're right. I've been unfair. You want to hear a funny coincidence? I'm heading out to Santa Barbara for a case. I could give you a ride to make it up to you. How does that sound?"

Officer Dick smiles widely. Desperate to get to his Vespa, Tommy casts aside any suspicions about the cop's sudden personality change. He decides that Officer Dick isn't the jerk he appeared to be and agrees to go with him. Lost again in Vespa dreaming, Tommy doesn't even ask for his Walkman back. He joyfully climbs into the back of the police car, and they set off on their way.

In the car, Officer Dick plays a cassette loudly. Annoyingly, it seems to have only two songs: Johnny Cash's "Ring of Fire" and Willie Nelson's "On the Road Again." Much to his chagrin, the words and melodies of both songs are slowly burned into Tommy's brain.

After driving more than two hours, Tommy gazes around at the scenery and the signs on the road. He realizes they are inland and moving away from the ocean. Tommy leans against the partition separating him from Officer Dick.

"Hey, Officer, I think you're going the wrong way. Santa Barbara is toward the ocean."

Officer Dick acts like he can't hear him. Tommy panics and tries to open the door, but it's a cop car . . . it's locked. The asshole cop glances backward and laughs uproariously. He speeds up, hitting 100 mph. Of course, no one's going to give him a ticket.

What a dick.

CHAPTER 7: BAKERSFIELD BLUES

Soundtrack: Manual Scan – "Nothing You Can Do"

OFFICER DICK'S CAR finally approaches its destination after more than four hours. Tommy sees a sign that reads, "Welcome to Bakersfield." Dear god, no, not Bakersfield.

"Officer Dick, why the fuck did you bring me here?"

"Two reasons, smart ass. First of all, I gotta follow up on a case. Secondly, you hurt my feelings."

Officer Dick laughs and pulls over. He lets Tommy out and speeds away, taking Tommy's Walkman with him. Tommy looks at a clock in the window of one of the stores: 7:30 p.m. Val's Vespa Emporium closes in an hour and he's at least two hours away from Santa Barbara.

Tommy wanders around until he finds the bus station. The next bus to Santa Barbara isn't until tomorrow. He's come too far to go back home with his tail between his legs. So, he meanders around Bakersfield. His conclusion after just a few minutes? What a shithole.

Around 9 p.m., he ends up at the local Swiftee Mart. He and some chick loading up in the liquor section are the only customers. Tommy rummages through the snacks, settling on potato chips, a pack of Life Savers, and a soda . . . the dinner of champions. Tommy notices the guy at the front counter seems nervous. He's clutching something tightly. Tommy gets closer. Shit, it's a shotgun!

"Hey, man, what's with the scary looking gun?" Tommy asks.

The clerk, whose eyes are bugging out, responds, "We got robbed last night! Don't you watch the news? Those damn Swiftee Mart bandits got us. Cleaned us out."

Wow, so Tommy's mom wasn't just talking out of her ass. Tommy passes the clerk his snacks.

"And some cigs too, man."

The clerk shakes his head.

"You don't look eighteen, kid."

Tommy sighs loudly.

"Come on, buddy, I turn eighteen in a month. I've had a really rough night. I'm stranded in the middle of this shitty place until the next bus comes in the morning. Do me a solid."

The clerk is unmoved by Tommy's plight, simply shaking his head again. Though he doesn't typically smoke, Tommy knows it calms people down in the movies, and he could use some calm right now. Tommy notices the woman in the store—now with a basket full of beer and vodka—is standing behind him. Embarrassed and not having the energy to argue any further, Tommy pays for his snacks and walks outside.

He sits on the sidewalk and digs into his chips voraciously. A couple minutes later, a cigarette pack lands in front of Tommy's feet. Startled, he turns around to see the woman from the Swiftee Mart. He checks her out: She's in her late forties and has wild eyes and dirty red hair. Her snug jeans and white tank top show off an impressively tight body.

She smiles at Tommy.

"I saw that you were having some trouble back there. I felt bad and wanted to help. The name's Cassidy."

Tommy opens the pack and takes out a cigarette.

"That's really cool of you, lady. Thanks."

Cassidy flirtatiously lights his cigarette for him and then lights one for herself. Tommy coughs. She puffs away like an old pro.

"So, kiddo, how did you wind up in this little corner of hell?"

Tommy, bored and sensing a sympathetic ear, proceeds to blather on about his tale of woe: his money problems, Stephanie breaking up with him and then having sex with David W. Tush, Officer Dick's dickishness, and his complicated quest to get a Vespa. By the end, even Tommy thinks he sounds like a whiny little baby and wants to slap the fuckin' shit out of himself. But before he can get to it, Cassidy puts her hand gently on his shoulder.

"Poor boy. You've had a rough time! Let me help you out."

After his experience with Officer Dick "helping" him, Tommy is understandably a bit hesitant to accept assistance from another stranger. But, what the heck, she seems pretty nice.

Cassidy hugs him affectionately.

"Why don't you wait here for a couple hours? I have a few stops to make, but after that I can take you some place where you can get a great night's rest. And then tomorrow, I can give you a ride to Santa Barbara, so you can get your scooter. It's on my way."

At midnight, Tommy finds himself still waiting by the Swiftee Mart for Cassidy to come back. Right when he is about to give up and find a park bench and a warm newspaper, he spots her strolling down the street.

"Sorry, hon, I was finishing up a deal. Come on, follow me."

She leads him to an old RV that looks like it's seen better days. She opens the door and leads him to the bed. It's not much, but Tommy feels grateful to have a warm place to sleep.

"Thank you, Cassidy. You've really saved me."

Cassidy kindly strokes Tommy's hair. Before he can ask her where she's going to sleep, she pushes him down onto the bed. What the hell? She takes off all her clothes. She's no Stephanie, but she looks incredible for her age. Her lean torso features a fierce dragon tattoo that spans the area between her breasts and her nether regions. As Tommy stares at his best view ever of a naked woman, he flashes back to all the hot older women he fantasized about on his delivery route. The difference is Cassidy isn't just flirting.

Cassidy straddles Tommy.

"I'm going to make you my love slave."

Tommy thinks that's a weird thing to say, but since it's his first time, he wonders if this is just regular sex talk. As she rips off his clothes, Tommy feels a pang of guilt and wonders if he should stop. But then he remembers: He has no girlfriend anymore. He can do whatever he wants.

They have sex. The kind of wild, violent, loud screwing that can only happen with a crazy person. Cassidy slaps Tommy around, bites him, pulls out clumps of his chest hair, and covers him in baby oil. Confused and frequently in pain, Tommy can't help thinking that this is very different than what he has been fantasizing about all these years.

The various kinds of sex finish around 6 a.m., when Cassidy finally lets Tommy rest. He is beyond exhausted and passes out as the sun rises.

A while later, Tommy startles awake to find that Cassidy is driving the RV. Tommy assumes she is going to Santa Barbara, so he allows himself to return to slumber.

At 2 p.m., Tommy wakes up to find that the RV has stopped at a campground somewhere. It definitely does not look like Santa Barbara. He wants to get dressed, but his clothes seem to be missing. He can't find his envelope of cash either! So, he walks out totally naked, covering up his manhood with his right hand. He walks up to Cassidy, who is smoking a cigarette.

"Hi," he mumbles sheepishly. "Where are we?"

Cassidy caresses his backside and kisses him.

"We're in Kettleman City. I had some deliveries to make."

Tommy is shocked. Kettleman City is even further away from the Vespa dealership!

"What happened to taking me to Santa Barbara? What about my Vespa?"

"Oh, sweet boy, I'm not going to Santa Barbara for a little scooter. It doesn't matter anyway. You're with me now and you're my little love machine. You go where I go."

Tommy starts to panic, realizing that Cassidy may have a screw loose. However, he thinks it's probably not a good idea to piss her off by saying he wants to leave.

"Can I have my clothes back?" Tommy asks.

Shaking her head, Cassidy responds, "No, you don't need them. You are as the lord intended you."

Okay, she really is insane. Tommy decides to play along until he can find a good opportunity to escape.

Cassidy spends the rest of the day and night making deliveries while Tommy sits naked in the back of the RV. Sometime after midnight, she comes to bed. Tommy fears another bout of crazy sex. He is covered in bruises and his entire body, including his dick, are sore. Cassidy moves toward the bed with a smile on her face. She sways side to side, clearly affected by something she swallowed, smoked, or sniffed at her last delivery.

"Get ready, lover! I'm going to fuck you so hard your dick falls off. I'm going to rip your ass up with my . . ."

She trails off and passes out right on top of the bed. As Cassidy snores loudly, Tommy realizes this is his chance to escape. He searches for the RV keys, but can't find them. He decides to make a run for it. He locates his envelope of cash and wallet, but still can't find his clothes. So, he takes the only pieces of clothing that he can find in the RV: a pair of granny panties, a tank top, and some flip flops.

He knows he looks frickin' ridiculous, but it's better than being butt naked. He runs at full speed down the road, hoping a change in his luck is coming.

CHAPTER 8: PIGS, CHICKENS, AND CULTS

Soundtrack: The Rain Parade – "What's She Done to Your Mind"

HOOFING IT IN the dark, Tommy dreads that Cassidy will wake up and somehow track him down. He spots a gas station in the middle of nowhere in the early morning hours. He stops and rubs his eyes, taking in this oasis in the middle of the desert.

As Tommy walks up, he sees a spectacular sight: twelve teens and twenty-somethings on scooters leaving the gas station in unison. With their fitted suits, minidresses, and cool haircuts, they're all so Mod that Tommy wants to cry. He is deeply envious.

On the last scooter is a Mod boy and a vision of beauty: the cutest, coolest girl Tommy has ever seen, with a white minidress, red knee-length boots, heavy eyeliner, and bobbed blonde hair. The Mod girl smiles and snaps a photo of Tommy on her vintage camera as they ride away.

Tommy adjusts his granny panties and tank top and starts to walk into the gas station when he hears laughing. Tommy looks over and sees a couple of blue collar guys in a truck guffawing like crazy. On the back of the truck are several pigs and a large cage with a number of chickens. The guys wave Tommy over.

As Tommy approaches, the blond guy in the passenger seat exclaims, "Hey, that's a nice outfit!"

Tommy shakes his head.

"I've had a weird few days."

The bald guy behind the steering sympathetically offers, "We've all been there, my friend. Need help getting somewhere?"

Though Tommy is wary of taking anyone else's help, he has no choice.

"I need to get to Santa Barbara."

"Come on in, we're going through there."

Apprehensively, Tommy climbs into the back. He is overcome with the smell of shit. Pigs and chickens really don't have the most pleasant odor. The blond guy grabs some sweatpants, a T-shirt, and a pair of sneakers and throws them to Tommy. Tommy puts them on. He doesn't exactly look fashionable, but at least he appears a bit more masculine.

Through the window in the back of the truck's cabin, the blue collar guys chat with Tommy during the nearly three-hour drive. The blond guy is named Jake and the bald guy is José. Their friends call them "J.J." They're gardeners and are delivering the pigs and chickens to make some extra money.

After hearing about Tommy's issues with Stephanie, José shakes his head.

"Man, she did you wrong. I once had this girl I loved more than anything. And one day, she told me she was leaving me for my own brother! She just ran out the front door and got into his car. I never saw either of them again!"

Tommy responds, "So, I guess that means you shouldn't trust women, eh?"

José turns around and stares right at Tommy. Tommy gets nervous, mainly because José's eyes should probably be on the road while he's driving.

José declares, "No, man! It just means she wasn't the woman for me! A few months later, I met this amazing girl. She turned out to be the best woman I ever met, and I married her. My point is that you should keep your eyes open. This Stephanie chick wasn't the one for you. But that doesn't mean there isn't a girl who's better for you out there."

Continuing the male bonding, the conversation turns to the subject of Tommy's money problems and mission to buy a Vespa.

Jake recounts, "A couple years ago, I was flat broke in the middle of Texas. A friend of mine called me from California and said he had a job for me on some work crew. So, the next day, I found myself hitchhiking across the country. I had some strange times, let me tell you! But it was the best decision I ever made, having the guts to just go on an adventure."

The talk with Jake and José reaffirms Tommy's obsessive quest to get a Vespa and his unwavering belief that it is the one thing that will change his entire life.

Around noon, Jake and José drop Tommy off in Santa Barbara. They give him their phone numbers and tell him to call if he ever wants to hang out or needs anything.

When they leave, Tommy immediately realizes that he smells like shit. And not the good kind either. We're talking pigs and chickens.

He proceeds to search for Val's Vespa Emporium but gets hopelessly lost. Exhausted, he sees a sign in front of a building that says, "Welcome, come in 24 hours!" Inside, Tommy finds an empty waiting room and a bathroom with—hallelujah!—a shower. He vigorously washes the stench from his body and his clothes.

Needing time for his clothes to dry, he conks out on the bench in the waiting room. It's not the most comfortable place to sleep, but

Tommy is so exhausted at this point that he could probably fall asleep standing up.

Around 4 p.m., Tommy wakes up to the sound of something buzzing close by. He glances up to see a pair of clippers descending toward his head. He dives out of the way, though the clippers still manage to shave a little patch from the side of his head. He looks around to find a group of bald cult members in loose, flowing clothes surrounding him. They're trying to shave his head! He looks over and sees that his clothes are gone. Even worse, his money has disappeared!

Tommy turns to the guy who looks like he's in charge.

"What the hell, man? What are you doing? Where's my stuff?"

The guru puts his hand over Tommy's heart.

"You must release your dependence on the material world. Live in your spirit, live in your heart. We shall help you, my friend."

Tommy hates this hippie-dippy shit.

"I don't need help. I just want my clothes and my money."

"The words you speak you do not truly believe. You want to stay here and be with us."

One of the other cult members steps forward. She's kind of hot despite the shaved head and shapeless clothes. Is this their attempt to seduce him? If he didn't have a Vespa to pick up, Tommy might have been enticed to stick around. As it is, he wants to get out of there. Fast.

"Thanks for the offer, but I have some place to be."

The guru shakes his head.

"No, you do not."

This ridiculous back-and-forth goes on for a while until it sounds like an argument a couple five-year-olds would have.

The guru finally presents an offer: "If you chant with us for a few hours, we will give you access to your material possessions. Then, you can choose whether you would like to stay or return to the cold, superficial world out there."

They hand Tommy a white gown, which he awkwardly puts on. Minutes later, he finds himself in a large room chanting words he doesn't understand and dancing around awkwardly. They then take him outside and do some more of this chanting and dancing by the front entrance. Tommy stands out from the rest because of his hair and the fact that he clearly doesn't know what he's doing. He makes noises that approximate the words the others are repeating. Tommy's strange gyrating causes him to run into the other cult members constantly, leaving many of them—and himself—pretty bruised.

After a few hours, he gets his money and clothes back. Aside from the small missing section of hair on the right side of his head, Tommy isn't too much worse for the wear after nearly being indoctrinated into a cult. Next stop: Val's Vespa Emporium.

CHAPTER 9: PARADISE . . . LOST

Soundtrack: The Untouchables – "Free Yourself"

IT'S AROUND 7 P.M. when Tommy manages to resume his search. With some dumb luck, he finally sees it: Val's Vespa Emporium. He stares at the rows of Vespas in the front, wondering if it is all just a mirage. He checks out the impossibly hot girls caressing shiny new Vespas out front. Of course, for Tommy, any girl touching a Vespa is hot.

Inside, the stereo system plays The Untouchables' "Free Yourself," as Tommy walks through the showroom and stares at the customers, all of them glistening and happy. There's a rich Mod guy decked in a beautiful tailored Italian suit as he buys a Vespa for his girlfriend, who poses seductively behind the handlebars. There's an older man announcing he has dreamed his whole life of getting a Vespa, as he hands over his credit card. Finally, there's a young director buying a Vespa for a new film he's shooting. Given his own desire to be a filmmaker, Tommy looks extra long at this guy, imagining himself in his place.

Amid the sea of beautiful people, Tommy feels a bit underdressed in his sweats. He goes to the front desk, where a clean-cut, dark-haired clerk greets him.

"Hello, sir. Welcome to Val's Vespa Emporium, home of the finest vehicle in the world . . . the Vespa! How can I help you, today?"

Tommy takes out his envelope of money and hands it the clerk.

"I'm Tommy Daniels and I'm here to pick up my Vespa. I ordered it through Gordy in Florida and he had it sent over here."

The clerk peruses a bunch of papers on his desk. He comes across a document and frowns at Tommy.

"Sir, I'm afraid I have some bad news. We just sold your Vespa."

Tommy's face drops.

"What? What do you mean you sold my Vespa? I put a deposit down with Gordy and everything! It was supposed to be here waiting for me!"

The clerk shakes his head.

"Your deadline to pick it up was the end of the day yesterday. When we didn't hear from you, we put it up for sale. Some guy and his girlfriend just bought it. They're right outside."

Tommy runs to the front entrance just in time to see his dream Vespa making a right turn onto the main street. On the back is the same hot Mod girl with the camera! Tommy is doubly jealous of the guy who bought his Vespa.

Tommy takes back his envelope of cash and holds back his tears.

The clerk, apologetic but annoyingly chirpy, rambles on: "You should inquire with Gordy in Florida about getting your deposit back. I know you're disappointed, sir, but we have many other Vespas here, each of them gorgeous emblems of Italian design and the embodiment of mankind's dreams of freedom."

Tommy grimaces at the clerk's ridiculously florid language. He checks out the other Vespas but most of them are out of his price range. The ones he can afford aren't what he wants. Anyway, his heart isn't into it. It's like when you're hung up on a girl. Even if you see or meet girls who are just as hot or even hotter, you don't want them; you're still thinking about the one that you really want, the one that you've wanted for what feels like forever. Tommy had found the perfect Vespa, but now it's lost forever.

Tommy is crushed. He literally looks five inches shorter, as he meanders out of the dealership, in a daze.

CHAPTER 10: THE MOST DANGEROUS GAME

Soundtrack: Agent Orange – "Everything Turns Grey"

TOMMY WANDERS AROUND Santa Barbara for a couple hours. Realizing he missed the last bus home, he searches for a place to crash. He really does not want to spend his precious money on a motel room.

He heads to the beach, looking for a quiet patch of sand. Unfortunately, there's a raucous party going on, featuring tons of rich kids downing beers and acting like assholes. This is the type of shit Tommy avoids like the plague back home. Nevertheless, Tommy could use a drink, so he decides to try to blend in.

As he approaches, he sees someone familiar. He moves closer to make sure it's him. Yep, it's the king of the assholes, David W. Tush! Tommy has the urge to beat the living crap out of David, just whale on him with all of his pent-up anger and frustration. But Tommy quickly realizes he is horribly outnumbered by David's friends. Plus, David is a lot bigger and stronger than he is.

Tommy fantasizes about having a group of Mod kids on Vespas with him. They could recreate some of those old Mods versus Rockers seaside brawls, the rich kids standing in for the Rockers. The fantasy brings a smile to Tommy's face before he walks away.

After roaming for another two hours, Tommy feels exhausted. He spots a large estate with a gargantuan house. As luck would have it, all the lights appear to be off and the side door has been left wide open. Tommy isn't one to break the law most of the time, but desperate times call for desperate measures. He athletically scales the fence and enters the house. Inside, he sees a comfy-looking couch and sprawls out, falling asleep almost instantly.

Around 10 a.m., Tommy's eyes snap open. He sees a man's face inches away from his own.

In a Cockney accent, the man indignantly asks, "What the fuck is this? Do you know who I am?"

Tommy shakes his head.

"I'm Ozzy Winstone."

He pauses for effect.

"Yes, *the* Ozzy Winstone."

It takes Tommy a few seconds but he recalls the name from an afternoon spent listening to old records with his dad. As they listened to an Ozzy Winstone LP, he remembers his dad talking about how Ozzy was a rock star who completely walked away from the spotlight at the height of his fame in the mid-70s.

Tommy stares at Ozzy's long, thinning hair and outfit, which is comprised of a silk robe, boxer shorts, and sandals.

Ozzy points at Tommy accusingly.

"Listen, bloke, I have you on camera breaking in and I have your fingerprints."

Ozzy flips open a wallet and reads the driver's license.

"I even have your wallet, Mr. Tommy Daniels."

Tommy realizes he is totally screwed. He considers running, but all of his money is in his wallet! He hears a police siren. He tries to plead with Ozzy.

"Man, you didn't have to call the cops! I just needed a place to sleep for a bit and couldn't find any other place that was free. I didn't think anyone was home!"

Ozzy shakes his head.

"I didn't call the cops."

At that moment, the cop car passes Ozzy's house with its siren blaring.

"But you *are* trespassing, Tommy boy. I won't press charges if you do a little something for me."

Tommy braces for the worst. This guy could be an old pervert. Still, not wanting to go to jail, he nods.

Ozzy, suddenly seeming almost bashful, paces back and forth and announces, "I rarely have any visitors, which I usually don't mind. But the thing is I like playing games and I hardly ever have anyone to play them with. So, what I want from you is to play a fun little game with me."

Despite the potentially perverse connotations of "fun little game," Tommy takes Ozzy's statement at face value and feels relieved that he only has to play a game with the old rocker.

Ozzy leads Tommy outside into a sprawling landscape filled with trees, assorted shrubbery, and a small lake. He then disappears for a few minutes and returns wearing head-to-toe black: leather jacket, T-shirt, jeans, and boots.

Ozzy asks, "Are you ready to play?"

He smiles, pulls out a rifle, and stares at Tommy with his crazed eyes.

Shit! Tommy's mouth drops and he tries to reason with Ozzy.

"Man, don't shoot me! I'm sorry for sneaking into your place."

Ozzy smiles darkly.

"Here are the rules. You run, I chase you. If you make it until noon, you win. If I catch you, well, you definitely lose. You get a five-minute head start. You should probably start running now."

Tommy freaks out. This guy is nuts! He wishes Ozzy had called the cops after all! With no other choice, Tommy starts running for his life.

Tommy decides to head for the trees that are behind the lake. He begins sprinting. As he makes his way around the lake, he trips and falls. To make matters worse, he rolls right into the water.

Tommy screams, "Mother fuckin' piece of shit!"

As he climbs back onto dry land, he hears Ozzy.

"Ready or not, here I come!"

Damn! Dripping wet, Tommy realizes that he is missing a shoe. It must have dropped in the lake. He takes off his other shoe and resumes running.

He makes his way into an avocado grove. He senses he is safe in the middle of all the trees, at least for the moment. He leans against a tree, panting badly. Suddenly, a rock-hard avocado falls off of a branch and lands right on Tommy's head, knocking him unconscious.

Tommy awakens a few minutes later to hear Ozzy's voice, now much closer.

"Oh baby, I'm getting close! I can smell you!"

The chase continues!

Is this really how I'm going to die?

Tommy asks himself this question, as he runs for his life through a massive grassy field. He hears footsteps getting closer and closer.

Sprinting faster than he ever has before, Tommy enters an area covered with winter creeper plants. His foot gets caught on the plants and he tumbles over. He pulls his foot with all his strength. He'd chew it off if he could. Just as he's about to extricate himself, he looks up. It's too late.

The mad man stands there smiling and pointing his rifle directly at Tommy.

"Too bad. You lose, man."

Tommy stands up. He wants to plead for his life, but no words come out. He closes his eyes. He flashes back to his life as it was two weeks ago: He had a hot girlfriend, less than a month until he started college, and the money to buy the Vespa of his dreams. And now, he faces what are probably his final moments on Earth.

A loud bang. Tommy feels a burning pain in his stomach. He opens his eyes and looks down.

All he sees is red . . .

But it doesn't quite look like blood. He touches the red liquid. Wait, is it . . . paint?

Tommy looks up at Ozzy, who bursts out laughing. Great, another dick.

In between fits of laughter, Ozzy repeats, "I'm sorry, mate. I'm sorry."

Tommy falls onto the ground, exhausted from the whole ordeal. It's tiring to believe you've been fatally shot with a bullet and then realize you've been shot with a fuckin' paint pellet.

Ozzy approaches and reaches his hand out to Tommy.

"Come on, Tommy, I'll fix you up some lunch and see what I can do to help you out."

As they walk back to the house, Ozzy starts laughing again.

"You should have seen the look on your face, kid! Are you sure you didn't wet yourself?

CHAPTER 11: TOMMY RIDES

Soundtrack: Small Faces – "All or Nothing"

IN BETWEEN BITES of a ham and egg sandwich, Tommy regales Ozzy with his life story: his obsession with Mod culture, fantasies of being a film director, inability to pay for college, unfaithful girlfriend, and near success in making his Vespa dreams come true.

Ozzy smiles.

"Shit, Tommy, you got a lot of crap going on! It's never easy being a teenager, is it? But, man, I rather be an absolute beginner like you than an old man like me."

Tommy responds, "You're not so old. My dad has some of your records and we listened to them once. They were pretty cool, from what I remember. Why don't you play anymore?"

Ozzy gets serious.

"A couple of my bandmates died. Drugs, drinking, all that rock 'n' roll shit. After they were gone, I didn't feel the music in the same way. I had enough money, so I just decided to stop and move out here."

Ozzy gets a little twinkle in his eye.

"But I'm thinking of getting started again. There's nothing cooler than an old man rockin' it hard on stage!"

Tommy laughs.

"Thanks for the sandwich, Ozzy, and for not actually killing me. I gotta be on my way. I guess I'm heading home."

Ozzy holds out his hand.

"Hold up, Tommy. Today might be your lucky day. Fuck knows, you're due for one. I have an old friend named Jimmy who lives close by. He was my road manager back in the day. A real solid bloke, not the asshole I am! Anyway, he's got an old scooter he wants to sell."

Tommy perks up.

"Really? Is it a Vespa?"

"I think so. Come on, I'll drive you over there."

Ozzy returns Tommy's wallet and leads him to the garage, which contains nearly a dozen expensive cars: classic Mercedes, BMW, and Porsche models, among others. Tommy's mouth drops. They get into a Range Rover and go on a short drive.

They arrive at a modest-looking house in a suburban neighborhood. Tommy can hear the song "All or Nothing" by Small Faces blaring inside. It's one of Tommy's favorite Mod tunes so he immediately feels at ease.

Ozzy knocks on the door. It opens and Ozzy slips inside. After a couple minutes, he comes back outside with a grin on his face.

"Alright, I told Jimmy your story. He says to come on in. I'm heading back home."

He hops into his Range Rover. He pulls down his window and hands Tommy a piece of paper.

"Here's my phone number, Tommy boy. If you're ever looking for a job, give me a ring. I'm starting work on a few projects and I might be able to use a smart kid like you."

After Ozzy drives off, Tommy heads into the house. As soon as he enters, he sees Jimmy. He is a skinny, white-haired English guy dressed fashionably in a tight suit. He is the epitome of Mod.

Jimmy looks Tommy up and down and states, "Brother, we're almost exactly the same size."

It's a weird thing to say, but Tommy is in such awe of how Mod Jimmy is that he barely notices.

Jimmy invites Tommy into the living room for some tea. Jimmy proceeds to delight Tommy with all sorts of stories from his Mod heyday in the 1960s. He talks about his first Italian suit, the jazz clubs he'd frequent, the bands he saw play, the girls he romanced, and the joys of being among the first group of teenagers with disposable income and independence. Tommy's favorite stories are, understandably, the ones about Jimmy's Vespa.

Jimmy tells Tommy about the Vespa's importance to his youth.

"I was just another fuckin' working class teenager in London . . . trying to get by, dreaming of pretty birds, working odd jobs. I wanted a Vespa so damn bad! My parents thought I was a fool! But it was the essence of cool. I saved up for a long time and the day I got it, I knew it would change my life. And fuck, if it didn't change it right away."

Grinning like crazy at Jimmy, Tommy knows he's acting like a lovesick teenage girl. If he could see his own face, he would probably slap it.

Jimmy continues, "On my first ride on my new Vespa, I spotted this girl, the nicest-looking bird I'd ever seen. I suddenly didn't want to bed every teenage girl in London. I just wanted her. I saw her get in a car. I followed that car every which way around London. I waved at her and smiled at her. Luckily, she smiled back."

"Did you ever get to actually meet her?"

"Fuck yeah! Her car eventually stopped at some shitty little pub. I followed her in and nothing was ever the same for me again. We were married a few months later. That was Olivia, the love of my life."

Jimmy wipes away a few tears. Before Tommy can ask questions, Jimmy gets started again.

"That Vespa didn't just change my life . . . it saved it once! Me and my old gang liked brawling back in the day, especially with those dirtbag Rockers. During one of those brawls, I was fighting this ferocious Rocker. I ain't ashamed to say that he was kickin' my ass. He shoved me right into my Vespa."

Tommy is riveted.

"Damn! Did you bust it?"

Jimmy shakes his head.

"No, man. But it hurt! Then, while I was on the ground, that shithead kept kicking me into my Vespa. I noticed the scooter was about to tip over, so I rolled out of the way. Then, it fell right onto that Rocker's leg! It pinned him to the ground and saved me from maybe getting killed."

Tommy slaps his hands together.

"Wow!"

"Once I had the upper hand, I beat the snot out of that Rocker and knocked him out. Once I calmed down, I felt bad about hurting him so bad. So, I dragged him over to the hospital before he bled to death."

Jimmy leans in.

"You want to know the strangest part?"

Tommy nods.

Jimmy chuckles, "Before I knew it, that Rocker and I became best friends! We're still friends to this day. You recently had the pleasure of his acquaintance."

Tommy's mouth drops.

"Ozzy?"

"Yeah! Me, the coolest Mod kid around became best mates with a Rocker. Can you believe it? A few years later, I was travelling around the world as Ozzy's road manager. It eventually led me to California, living the life of luxury. No more shitty London weather for me!"

Tommy smiles.

"That's a great story."

"The point is that I was a lot like you. I was obsessed with being Mod and getting a Vespa. Everyone thought I was crazy. But I knew myself and what my life needed better than any of them, and I never gave up. Everything good in my life came because I followed my gut. I got that fuckin' Vespa."

Jimmy walks Tommy to the front of the house.

"Wait in front of the garage."

Tommy stands there, still absorbing all the amazing stories. A few minutes pass. Suddenly, the garage door opens.

When Tommy sees what's inside, his eyes open wide, so wide they feel like they might pop out of his head. Angels singing in his head, he steps into the garage. There it is . . . the most perfect Vespa Tommy's ever seen. It's a silver Vespa GS. It looks just like the one Sting rode in *Quadrophenia*!

Not moving his eyes from the Vespa, Tommy inquires, "How much?"

Jimmy responds, "What've you got?"

"I have around two thousand."

"Give me eighteen hundred. You need some gas money."

Tommy hands Jimmy the money. Jimmy hands him the keys. Though Tommy is beyond happy, he can't help wondering why Jimmy would give up something that clearly means so much to him.

He asks, "Why would you ever sell a Vespa this amazing?"

Jimmy shakes his head.

"My wife, my dear Olivia passed away a few months ago. When I get on my Vespa, all I can remember is her arms around me, riding through the streets of London and riding around here. I think back to that day I first bought the Vespa and saw her beautiful face for the first time. It's too much."

He gazes wistfully at the Vespa and puts his hand on the seat.

"I want to pass it on to someone who can love it and appreciate it, like I did. Maybe it'll help your dreams come true too."

Before going back inside, Jimmy hands Tommy a box.

"Good luck, Tommy."

Tommy waves goodbye to Jimmy, then looks down at the box. There is a note attached to it.

It reads, "I hope this beautiful old girl takes you as far as she has me. From one Vespa aficionado to another, here are some new threads to go with your new wheels. Remember: clean living under difficult circumstances."

There is an additional message at the bottom of the note: "P.S. You smell like pig shit for some reason."

Tommy opens the box. Inside, he finds the most flawless Mod suit he has ever seen. It's gray, Italian, and impeccably tailored. Jimmy even included a shirt, thin tie, desert boots, and vintage military parka. Tommy gets dressed with a smile on his face. Everything is a perfect fit.

There is a mirror in the garage. Tommy checks himself out. He is quite certain he has never looked cooler or more Mod in his entire life.

Awash with confidence and the sense that anything is possible now, Tommy gets on his scooter. He takes a moment to admire its beauty and marvel at the shocking fact that it belongs to him, Tommy Daniels!

Tommy remembers that there is a Vespa rally the next day in L.A. So, he turns on his Vespa and heads south.

On the road, Tommy screams at the top of his lungs. He feels fuckin' orgasmic. His dream, once so far away, has finally come true.

CHAPTER 12: HAPPY INTERLUDE: EMMY AND THE MOD KIDS

Soundtrack: The Plimsouls – "Now"

TOMMY TAKES IN the fresh California ocean breeze as he rides his Vespa toward L.A. In a coincidence that confirms that his life has taken a happy turn, Tommy spots a group of nearly thirty Mod kids on scooters. It's the same group he saw yesterday but it has grown much larger since then. They're probably on their way to the scooter rally he's heading for, so he follows them. They all eventually stop at a little burger joint next to a truck stop.

That's where he sees her again . . . the Mod girl with the camera from the gas station in Kettleman City and the Vespa dealership in Santa Barbara. She looks even hotter up close. Blonde, thin, a little dangerous. Basically, she's every teenager's fantasy girl. Even better for Tommy, she's into Vespas and Mod culture.

Tommy and the girl make eye contact.

He stutters, "Uh, I like Vespas. You're Mod. Me too. That's cool."

The girl laughs—in a nice way—at his dumb greeting. She shakes his hand.

"Hi, my name is Emmy."

Tommy keeps shaking her hand and staring into her impossibly gorgeous brown eyes.

Emmy smiles and asks, "What's your name?"

Breaking out of his trance, he responds, "Tommy. My name is Tommy Daniels."

"Nice meeting you, Tommy. Didn't I see you at a gas station yesterday? You looked pretty funny. You were wearing a tank top and some really unflattering underwear."

Tommy turns bright red. Shit, she remembers! Not the best first impression to make.

Tommy responds, "Yeah, umm, that was me. Some strange stuff happened and I had to wear some clothes that weren't mine."

Emmy laughs.

"Well, you look much better now! That's an amazing suit."

"Thanks. I just got it."

Tommy and Emmy stand around awkwardly for a few seconds.

Emmy finally interrupts the silence: "So . . . we're all riding around today, enjoying the weather. Then, we're going to camp out at night before going to a scooter rally in L.A. tomorrow. Wanna join us?"

Tommy smiles.

"Absolutely!"

Emmy heads back to the Mod boy she rode in with. She climbs onto the back of his Vespa. All the Mod kids hit the road. Tommy follows.

As he rides down the highway with them, Tommy feels more at home than he ever has. Finally, a group of people who value the same things he does. He no longer feels like he was born twenty years too late and on the wrong continent. La Jolla seems like a bad dream.

Throughout the ride, Tommy makes sure to stay close to Emmy. He passes her playfully on several occasions with his Vespa. Emmy smiles and snaps photos of Tommy from the back of the Mod boy's scooter.

The group eventually stops at a campground outside of L.A. Emmy introduces Tommy to the guy she's riding with.

"Hey, Aston, this is Tommy. Tommy, meet Aston."

Aston shakes Tommy's hand, glares a bit at him, and then walks away to hang out with his friends. Tommy and Emmy grab some sodas and walk around the campground, as a boom box plays the Mod classic "Now" by the Plimsouls.

They're both overtly nervous, but they soon gather the courage to tell each other about their lives. Sitting around a campfire, Tommy tells her about Stephanie, his family's money problems, his obsession with Mod culture and Vespas, and the bland world of La Jolla. Emmy proves very sympathetic.

"So, do you have friends?"

"Sure. My best friend was Stephanie, but I have a few others. My favorite person to hang out with is this author I deliver pills to for the pharmacy. His name is Dr. Harvey."

Emmy's eyes open wide.

"*The* Dr. Harvey?"

Tommy doesn't generally like showing off that he's friends with a famous author, but he doesn't mind impressing Emmy.

"Yep. He's a great guy. After I gave all my money to my dad to pay for rent, Dr. Harvey gave me the money to buy my Vespa. He said I inspired his newest book and this was his way of paying me back for my help."

Emmy smiles and leans back, gazing up at the stars. Tommy takes the opportunity to study the beautiful girl who has suddenly appeared in his life. She is wearing a minidress, exposing her impossibly long legs. Tommy can't help thinking they're the nicest legs he's ever seen. He sees her shiver, so he takes off his parka and slips it on her.

"Thanks, Tommy. That's very sweet."

She puts her hands through her hair.

"So, what do you want to study in college?"

"I want to make movies. I'd like to become a director and make a movie showing Mod culture in California today and how cool it is. It's so much more real than anything in my hometown."

Emmy nods.

"It's funny. You're into the moving image, and I'm all about the still image."

Tommy grins at the connection they share.

"What kind of photos do you take?"

Emmy caresses her camera.

"I take photos of everything. Mainly people I meet or see. Life is so fast. Every moment just passes by so quickly. We rarely have time to sit and think about things. That's why I take photos. The photos I like are the ones that capture something about the person, something meaningful and deep that you may not even learn from talking to them."

That's it, Tommy thinks, I'm in love. She's not only the most beautiful girl Tommy has ever seen, she's deep.

"Do you wanna study photography in college?"

She suddenly appears very upset.

"I don't know. My dad is trying to force me to go to UCLA and study business."

"What does your mom think about that?"

Emmy takes a deep breath.

"My mom died a few years ago. Cancer. I love my dad, but he tries to control every aspect of my life! He runs some consulting company. I don't really understand what he does, but he does it really well and makes a lot of money. He would love for me to work with him and eventually take over. I love him, but it's just not who I am."

Tommy gazes into her eyes.

"Taking photos for a living would make you happy?"

"Creativity makes me happy. I take photos and design clothes. This outfit I'm wearing . . . I made it myself."

Tommy's mouth drops in disbelief. He looks at her perfectly Mod yellow minidress and her matching yellow shoes. He assumed that her outfit was vintage.

Emmy continues, "I wouldn't be happy sitting in an office looking at numbers. I want to be out in the world with people, being inspired by them and then creating art, whether it's photos or fashion."

"Have you thought about going to art school?"

Emmy smiles widely.

"That's exactly what I want to do! I've applied for late enrollment in an art school in L.A. I have an interview in a few days. But if I get accepted and go, my dad said he won't give me a dime for tuition."

"You would be in the same boat as I am, having to pay for your own school. But it's not the worst thing. You'd be following your dreams. Better to make yourself happy than your dad."

Emmy nods, considering Tommy's words. Tommy senses an opening to ask a question that's really been eating away at him.

"So, who is Aston exactly?" Wishfully, he adds, "Is he your brother or something?"

Emmy hesitates, then responds, "Technically, he's my boyfriend. We've been dating for a while, but we're more friends than anything at this point. I feel like we've broken up in our heads already, but neither of us has actually said the words."

Emmy shivers and moves her hands closer to the fire.

"Aston is kind of an asshole anyway. He is obsessed with himself and how he looks. His goal in life is to become even richer than his dad. He doesn't understand why I want to go to art school."

Tommy is bummed out. He respects the sanctity of teenage relationships, no matter how rocky they are. He can't kiss a girl who has a boyfriend, especially when he is hanging out in the same campground.

"If you don't want to be with him, why are you riding around with him, buying a Vespa with him, and camping with him?"

She sighs loudly.

"Keep in mind I'm here talking to you rather than hanging out with him. The truth is, living in Newport Beach I'm bored out of my mind most of the time. For all of Aston's faults, he's the only guy around who knows anything about being Mod and appreciates my unusual fashion choices."

Tommy admits to himself that if there was some girl in La Jolla who was into Mod culture, he probably would have tried to date her, even if she wasn't the greatest human being.

Tommy asks her, "Why are you so into Mod culture?"

Emmy grins.

"It's cool. It's young. Compare Mod clothes to the ridiculous clothes everyone wears these days. There's personality and energy in the clothes and in the people who are truly Mod. It's an attitude, a way of life. And the Vespa . . . has there been any other vehicle that is more beautiful, that expresses an entire movement in its very being?"

Tommy couldn't have said it better himself. The two of them stay up late talking about the awesomeness of Mod culture and Vespas. They flirt plenty, but nothing physical happens. Tommy knows the pain of your girl hooking up with someone else (he curses the name

"Tush" whenever he gets the chance). He isn't about to put Aston through that, even if he is a total dickwad.

Despite the lack of any making out, it is the greatest night of Tommy's life, capping off the best day he's ever had.

CHAPTER 13: EASY COME, EASY GO

Soundtrack: The Chords – "Maybe Tomorrow"

TOMMY IS A heavy sleeper. By the time he wakes up, all the Mod kids are starting up their scooters and leaving. No one bothered to wake him up! He spots Emmy arguing with Aston while pointing in Tommy's direction.

Tommy gets on his Vespa to follow them as they ride off. But it won't start. He tries again and again. He checks to see if anything is busted. Tommy's not exactly mechanically inclined, but everything appears to be in order. Then, he looks at the Vespa's gas meter . . . empty. Goddamnit, someone has siphoned out his gas!

Tommy watches as the scooters all leave. When Aston sneers at him, it becomes pretty clear who stole his gas. It appears he wasn't as cool as he seemed with Tommy spending time with his girlfriend. Emmy looks at Tommy sadly and waves as she rides away on the back of Aston's scooter.

Tommy asks a passerby how far it is to the nearest gas station. Learning that it's five miles away, Tommy sighs and begins pushing his Vespa. It is ridiculously hot, so Tommy ties his parka and jacket around his waist. Sweat drips from every inch of his body, even from places he didn't know he could sweat. As he makes his way, he gazes up and sees a vulture circling. That's never a good sign.

At the gas station, Tommy fills up his Vespa's tank. He then sets off for L.A. Though the Mod kids (well, at least Aston) stole from him, he wants to rejoin them. If nothing else, he wants to see Emmy again.

Tommy accelerates down the road, feeling like a real speed demon. Of course, since he is riding a Vespa, he doesn't actually go all that fast. He gets passed by several station wagons, an old bald guy in a Porsche, a giant Cadillac, and what looks like a converted old Ford Model-T. He approaches the entrance to the freeway.

Out of nowhere, Tommy hears a police siren. Before Tommy can even react, the police car literally drives circles around him, seemingly mocking his unimpressive rate of speed. Tommy and the cop both pull over. Tommy can't believe his luck. He is in a hurry! Plus, he can't afford to pay for a ticket.

The cop walks up and, god almighty, it's Officer Dick! When he realizes it's Tommy, he gets a goofy grin on his face.

"Hey, you made it out of Bakersfield!"

Tommy wants to curse him out. It's Officer Dick's fault all of the bad shit from the last few days happened. Tommy could have quietly gotten on his bus, bought his Vespa, and been home four days ago. But he doesn't want to give Officer Dick any more excuses to make his life miserable.

Tommy sheepishly asks, "Officer, what did I do wrong?"

Dick smiles.

"You don't know how to read."

"Huh?"

Officer Dick points to a street sign that lists the speed limit as 35 mph.

"Kid, you were speeding!"

Tommy is incredulous.

"Speeding? It's a *Vespa*!"

Officer Dick shakes his head.

"You had it revved up to 37 mph, hot shot! You were endangering the lives of the citizens of this fine country."

Tommy is fuming. But then, he realizes something that could make the whole situation go away.

"Hey, Officer Dick, you're a La Jolla police officer, right? Well, that means you can't give me a speeding ticket since we aren't even in the same county!"

Officer Dick fondles his mustache for a good five seconds.

"Wow, kid, you're smarter than you look. A real Einstein lurking in there, eh? You're absolutely right. I can pull you over, but I can't give you a ticket. Whatever will I do?"

As Officer Dick paces back and forth in mock panic, a California Highway Patrol motorcycle pulls up. A mustached, fat cop (really, he could be Officer Dick's brother) walks up.

Officer Dick introduces Tommy to the CHP Officer.

"Kid, this is my good friend Officer Dool. I radioed him a while ago. I think *he* can give you a ticket."

Officer Dick turns to Officer Dool.

"Be careful, Carl, this kid has some real attitude."

Officer Dool smiles at Officer Dick, then scowls at Tommy.

"You've been causing my buddy some problems, have you? We police officers stick together, especially when it comes to taking on hooligans like you."

Tommy can't stand it.

He bursts out, "You guys get off on making trouble for kids like me. Just because I'm a teen doesn't mean you should single me out. I was only going two miles over the speed limit. You're both dicks!"

Officer Dool coolly radios something in, then takes Tommy's driver's license and writes him a ticket.

"I'm afraid you'll be walking home, kid."

Tommy is confused.

"What?"

"Yep, we're going to have to impound that Vespa. It'll teach you to have respect for those in authority. You can pick it up at the police impound lot a couple miles from here. There will be a small fine."

Tommy considers getting back on his scooter and trying to outrun his nemesis and his asshole friend. But he doesn't want to end up in jail. That would be a hard one to explain to his parents and who knows what that would end up costing his family in fines and legal fees.

So, he watches sadly as a tow truck arrives and takes away his Vespa. Tommy is left stranded.

After hoofing it for two miles, Tommy makes it the impound lot in the Podunk town. A large, unpleasant looking woman guards the front desk. She looks like she would fit right in at the DMV.

"What do you want?"

Tommy tries to be extra polite.

"Miss, my Vespa was impounded by one of your cops. Please, I'd like to pick it up."

"Sure, you can take it. But first you got to pay the fine."

She checks her papers.

"It'll be two hundred dollars!"

Tommy is flabbergasted. He counts his money. He doesn't have enough.

"How about a hundred?"

The disagreeable woman stands up.

"Does this look like a flea market? You violated the law. This is the penalty. Either pay the full fine or get out. Don't be wasting my time!"

Tommy walks out. Could this day get any worse?

He is determined: He will get his Vespa out of that impound lot, even if it means breaking the law!

After spending the afternoon hanging out at the local Swiftee Mart drinking soda and eating some peanuts, Tommy returns to the impound lot around 8 p.m., when it's dark. Looking through the fence, he spots his Vespa in a corner.

Tommy gets a running start and hurls himself at the fence, grabbing on somewhere in the middle. He pulls himself up the rest of the way. As he begins to climb down the interior of the fence, things hit a snag. Literally. His parka gets stuck on the top of the fence. Try as he might, he can't detach himself.

He has an idea. He lets go of the fence, hoping his weight will help release him from the grip of the evil enclosure. Initially, there is no effect. Tommy just hangs there, suspended by his parka like some kind of angel floating above the police impound lot. Finally, with sufficient kicking, punching, and pulling, he unfastens himself from the fence. In the process, the fence tears his jacket in two, basically destroying it. To top things off, another protrusion tears his pant leg from top to bottom on his way to the ground. In other words, Tommy could really use a tailor.

Inside the impound lot, Tommy runs to his Vespa and hugs it. He realizes this might seem pathetic, but love is love. In a day full of misfortunes, Tommy finally has a stroke of luck when he finds the Vespa's keys just sitting there on the seat. He rolls his Vespa quietly to the impound lot's chained gate. He ponders ramming the gate open, but he's not sure he can get enough speed or brute force from his Vespa to do that.

He searches for something to cut the chains on the gate. In another instance of dumb luck, Tommy spots a pair of bolt cutters on the ground. He uses them on the chain and a minute later he rolls his Vespa onto the street. He turns it on and hits the road.

Tommy's parka is in tatters and his suit is looking pretty sorry, but he's happy to have his Vespa back. Fearful that the cops are searching for him, he gets lost in the town for a while before managing to get back on the road to L.A.

On the highway, the harrowing day catches up to Tommy pretty quickly and he finds himself getting very sleepy. He pulls over at a random Swiftee Mart for some coffee. As he pays for a scaldingly hot cup of joe, Tommy peers at the cashier. His face has gone white as he holds Tommy's five-dollar bill in his hand.

Tommy asks, "Can I have my change, please?"

The cashier puts his hands into the air. Tommy turns around and sees what has the cashier's attention: two bandits wearing facemasks and holding guns. The bigger bandit approaches the cashier, pistol first.

"Give me the cash and no one gets hurt!"

The cashier dumps all the money into a bag that the smaller bandit holds out. While they are distracted, Tommy inches backward and ducks down behind the snack aisle. Hiding may not be the bravest move, but Tommy has no hero complex. He rather not get killed.

The bandits take the money and sprint outside. Tommy watches from inside as the smaller bandit sees Tommy's Vespa and pauses.

As the bigger bandit drives away in a van, the other one stays behind, fiddling with the scooter. Tommy nervously wonders what the hell the bandit could be doing to his prized possession.

Hearing the engine start, Tommy realizes the bandit just hotwired his Vespa! Tommy's fear subsides and he runs out of the Swiftee Mart.

"No! That's mine! Goddamnit!"

Tommy chases after the bandit, but he and the Vespa are gone. Tommy falls to his knees on the sidewalk, tears filling his eyes.

A minute later, a cop responds to the call for help. When Tommy looks up, he sees him: his nemesis, the one and only Officer Dick. Tommy wonders if there are any other fucking cops in all of Southern California. He thinks about bolting out of there, but Officer Dick has already spotted him.

"Kid, what are you doing here? Are you following me or something?"

Tommy considers telling him about his Vespa getting stolen, but then Officer Dick would find out Tommy snatched it from the impound lot without paying.

Tommy responds, "What are *you* doing here? Aren't you a La Jolla cop?"

Officer Dick's eyes narrow. Then, he sighs.

"I've been chasing everywhere after those damn Swiftee Mart bandits. If I catch them, they'll be forced to promote me to detective. Finally!"

Clearly upset that he missed the bandits again, Officer Dick goes inside to interview the store clerk and canvass the scene for any evidence. Tommy sits on the sidewalk silently, feeling sorry for himself. A few minutes later, Officer Dick leaves the Swiftee Mart and saunters up to Tommy.

Sounding unusually sympathetic, Officer Dick announces, "Hey, kid, let me help you out. It's been four days since I spotted you in La Jolla. Have you been on the road this entire time?"

Tommy nods.

"Here's some change. Why don't you call your parents and let them know you're on your way home."

Officer Dick takes a quarter out of his pocket and hands it to Tommy. He realizes he probably should have called his parents days ago, but he wanted to figure things out on his own. Feeling defeated, Tommy walks over to the nearby payphone and dials home.

His mom picks up the phone and frantically screams, "Tommy! Oh, my god! We thought something horrible happened to you! We were so worried. We thought maybe you and Stephanie had taken a long weekend trip together. But then we called her house and she said she hadn't seen you in a long time. We reported you missing yesterday!"

His mom goes on about how worried they were for another minute or so. Tommy barely says a word, so dejected by everything that has happened. Officer Dick grabs the phone from him.

"Ma'am, I will get your son home safely, I promise you. I am an officer of the law and my duty is sacred to me."

Though Tommy doesn't trust Officer Dick as far as he can throw him (and that isn't very far, given his girth), he is too exhausted to doubt his motives. He gets into the back of the police car and Officer Dick drives him home.

PART 3: MOD AS HELL

CHAPTER 14: HOME, DEPRESSING HOME

Soundtrack: The Question – "Getting Through"

IT'S 10 A.M. AND Tommy is in his bed at home, staring at the ceiling mournfully. He takes stock of his life: His parents are pissed at him, Stephanie is long gone, and Emmy, the girl of his dreams, is god-knows-where. Worst of all, the Vespa that he always dreamed about belonged to him for what felt like just a moment. After all the money and time he spent, he is left with nothing to show for it.

He picks up a magazine from the floor of his bedroom. He flips through it and stares at photos of scooters. He puts his hands on the pages, trying to somehow touch the Vespas represented in the pages. He sheds more than a few tears. It's a pretty pitiful scene, capping five days of similar self-loathing bullshit.

Tommy's dad walks into his room with a determined expression on his face.

"Son, you've got to stop this. I know it's not always easy to look on the bright side of things."

From his bed, Tommy glares at his father, who continues, "A Vespa isn't everything, even if it does mean a lot to you. You have less than two weeks until you start college. You are lucky to have the chance to get an education."

Tommy glances at his father's face. He can tell he is trying to help. But he just doesn't feel hopeful.

"Dad, what about the money? Even if I work, things are going to be super tight. I don't know if I'll be able to handle all of it. What if I don't do well in school? What if I crumble under all the pressure?"

Tommy's dad puts on a smile.

"Tommy, I know I haven't always done right by you, and I haven't always been able to support you and your mother and give you all the things you deserve. But I promise I will help you put together the money for your tuition. If you go to college and get a good education, maybe you won't end up like me, always scraping by and disappointing your family."

Tommy doesn't respond. His dad goes to the bed and pulls Tommy up. He gives him a bear hug.

"Son, I love you. Please do me a favor. Just get out of the house, even for an hour, and do something. Sitting around staring at the walls of your bedroom isn't healthy. Get some fresh air, see some friends."

Tommy nods. Maybe his dad is right and getting out of the house will help. Of course, the last time he interacted with the world outside things didn't exactly go well.

CHAPTER 15: REVENGE . . . SWEET, ANGRY REVENGE

Soundtrack: The Three O'Clock – "I Go Wild"

TOMMY HAS AN hour to kill before he can return to the sweet embrace of his bedroom. He doesn't want to see anyone he knows, so he heads to the local Swiftee Mart for a slushy. Those rich assholes he went to school with wouldn't hang out at a place as pedestrian as a Swiftee Mart. Plus, maybe the sugar will artificially lift his spirits.

He gets to the door of the mart and pushes. It's locked. Then, Tommy sees the sign on the door: "REALLY big waves, gone surfing!" Dumb asses.

Things quickly get weirder. He sees two guys inside the Swiftee Mart moving behind the register. Tommy is pissed: Why put up the bullshit sign if you're still in there? He knocks several times, but they ignore him. Fuckers!

He turns around and moves toward the parking lot. As he walks past a truck, he spots a scooter. It's a silver Vespa GS. Funny, it kind of looks like his Vespa. He gets closer. It *is* his Vespa! He glances back at the men in the Swiftee Mart. Tommy realizes they're wearing masks. It's the two bandits! Tommy is enraged beyond all belief.

Tommy flashes back to his traumatic quest for the Vespa: Officer Dick leaving him in Bakersfield, Cassidy and the frightening sex, running away in granny panties, the pig and chicken shit, the cult, the

Vespa he reserved being driven away from Val's Vespa Emporium, being hunted by Ozzy and believing he was about to die, the Mod kids ditching him, Officer Dick and his friend impounding his Vespa, and, finally, the Swiftee Mart bandits stealing his Vespa.

Anger fills Tommy's being and he yearns for revenge. He spots a skateboarder napping by the side of the store, probably stoned out of his mind. Tommy nabs his skateboard and waits outside the door of the Swiftee Mart.

The bandits come out laughing about how easy the score was. Tommy sees red. As the first bandit moves past him, Tommy whacks him in the back of the head with the skateboard. He goes down. Hard. While the second bandit stares at his friend in shock, Tommy takes the skateboard and slams it into his stomach. He bends over in pain. Tommy proceeds to hit both bandits repeatedly with the skateboard and kick them all over the place. He even rips off their masks. In short, he beats the living shit out of them until they are unconscious.

Ecstatic over his victory, Tommy struts toward his Vespa as a police siren blares in the distance. Tommy takes out the keys to the Vespa from his pocket. He's been carrying them around, even though he never expected to see the Vespa again. He is inches away from his dream machine, when he hears tires screeching.

Tommy looks down the street and sees a police car approaching. But, it's going way too fast. It's out of control! With only a moment to react, Tommy dives out of the way. The cop car screeches, slides, and then smashes right into Tommy's Vespa.

Tommy pulls himself from the pavement. He scrutinizes the scene of the accident. The cop car is dented, but the Vespa . . . dear god, the Vespa. It is crushed beyond any hope of repair. It's a heap of barely recognizable mangled machinery.

Tommy gets a crazy look on his face, as he wonders, *Am I fuckin' cursed?* The cop gets out of the car. And guess who? Officer Dick! Tommy loses it. He starts yelling nonsense. He sounds like Stallone at the end of the first Rambo movie: scarred by the memories of too many battles.

Officer Dick sees Tommy's psychotic behavior, then spots the two beaten men on the ground. He gets a smile on his face, clearly having reached an epiphany.

"You're totally bonkers, kid, aren't you? This is the second time I've caught you at one of these Swiftee Marts right after a robbery. I think I have you red-handed this time, you damn Swiftee Mart bandit! Where's your partner?"

He handcuffs Tommy, who resists, and then shoves him into the back of the police car. Tommy watches as Officer Dick moves to help the downed bandits, checking their pulses. Two blond skateboarders in backwards baseball caps approach.

The first skateboarder explains, "Hey, officer, man. Why are you arresting that kid? He's a total hero!"

Officer Dick furrows his brow.

"What the hell are you prattling on about? He has robbed multiple Swiftee Marts and he beat the darn life out of these two young men!"

The second skateboarder cuts in, "No, man. You really suck at your job. Those two assholes down there were robbing the place. Look!"

The skateboarder points to the masks on the ground next to the bandits and the cash protruding from the duffle bag that's by their feet. Officer Dick's face drops as he realizes the truth about the situation. He handcuffs the two unconscious bandits and returns to his car. He radios an ambulance for the bandits. Then, he opens the back door, where Tommy sits, in too much shock to say anything.

Noticeably embarrassed, Officer Dick admits, "Hey, kid, I was wrong. It turns out I misread the situation."

He opens Tommy's handcuffs. Still in a stupor, Tommy stumbles over to the remains of the Vespa and falls to his knees. He salvages one piece: a side mirror. He stares at it longingly.

With tears in his eyes, he moans, "It's all I ever wanted."

Seeing Tommy stare at his busted Vespa, Officer Dick offers some sympathy: "I know what it's like to want something so bad and have it be just out of reach."

Officer Dick puts his hand on Tommy's shoulder.

"When I was your age, the only thing I wanted in the world was a shiny red Corvette. I spent all my time looking at magazines with pictures of Corvettes and dreaming of how my life would change if I got one."

Officer Dick looks into the distance, smiling faintly.

"And there was Laurie Lorimar, this beautiful redhead I was in love with but never had the guts to talk to. One day, this rich jock drove up to school in a gorgeous red Corvette. Laurie smiled this amazing smile and just ran to him. Before I knew it, they were dating. A few years later, they were married."

Officer Dick kneels down next to Tommy.

"Guys like you and me, we don't always get what we want. We don't always get the pretty girl, the nice car, or the scooter. But we have to keep working hard and trying our best. Because you never know when your life might turn around."

He helps Tommy up and shakes his hand.

"And, hey, kid, you're a real hero."

Tommy appreciates his one-time nemesis being so kind to him, but he feels totally unable to speak. How can he, when his dreams are in pieces right in front of him?

CHAPTER 16: A FUNERAL AND AN UNEXPECTED TURN OF EVENTS

Soundtrack: Secret Affair – "My World"

TOMMY STANDS ALONE in the backyard. He picks up a shovel and starts digging. Once the hole is a few feet deep, he drops the shovel. He takes out a small box. He opens it and removes the Vespa's side mirror. He places it into the hole. He forlornly piles dirt on.

Recovering from this pathetic little funeral, Tommy goes to his room and stretches out on his bed. He turns on his TV, an ancient-looking black-and-white set. He likes to leave on the local news and close his eyes when he wants to zone out from the world.

After a few minutes, one news story catches his attention. The newscaster states, "In perhaps our most interesting story of the day, a La Jolla teenager foiled the Swiftee Mart bandits who have plagued Southern California these past few months."

Tommy sits up in bed and stares at the TV. They show some footage captured by one of the nearby security cameras of Tommy beating the hell out of the bandits. They even have video of Officer Dick crushing the Vespa and Tommy tearfully gazing at the corpse of his lost love. Tommy turns off the TV, presses play on his cassette deck, and slams back onto his bed as Secret Affair's "My World" commences.

Several minutes later, the doorbell rings. After a few moments, Tommy's mom calls him to the door. Like a zombie, he drags himself downstairs and to the front entrance of the house.

"What is it, Mom?"

Tommy is startled to find his mom and dad standing with Officer Dick, an older man from the police department, and some guy in a fancy suit. Tommy's mom and dad both smile and push him toward the men.

Tommy's dad announces, "Tommy, these men have some pressing business with you."

Tommy wonders if the cops are going to charge him for assaulting the bandits or perhaps they found out that he stole the Vespa out of the police impound lot. The older cop steps forward.

"I'm Stan McCoy, Captain of the La Jolla police department. I'd like to commend you for your heroic acts yesterday. All of the police departments in Southern California have been after those bandits for some time. Frankly, I feel a little envious that you got to beat the heck out of those monsters."

Tommy is still nervous, but manages a little smile.

Captain McCoy continues, "My friend Officer Richard here has a few words he'd like to say to you."

Officer Dick steps forward awkwardly, like a little kid whose parents found out he did something bad and are making him apologize.

"Mr. Daniels, I drove recklessly. I destroyed your scooter and endangered your life. Just as bad, I mistook you for a criminal, handcuffing you and shoving you in the back of my car. For all of my actions that offended and harmed you, I apologize and hope you can forgive me and not think ill of the La Jolla Police Department."

Tommy stares into Officer Dick's pleading eyes and can tell that he hasn't told his captain about all the other stuff he did that hurt

Tommy, such as leaving him in Bakersfield and getting his Vespa impounded for speeding. But Tommy feels bad for the guy: It's clear he's been yelled at plenty in the last day and he is probably the butt of countless jokes for demolishing the Vespa. So, he doesn't want to make things worse.

"Thank you for your apology, Officer Richard."

Officer Dick proceeds to take something out of his pocket. It's Tommy's Walkman!

"Umm, Mr. Daniels, I think you left this in my car."

Tommy looks at the Walkman and remembers how happy he was to get it from Stephanie. That day seems like such a long time ago. Tommy decides he's better off not holding onto things from the past.

"Officer Dick, please keep it. I don't need it anymore."

Officer Dick smiles.

Tommy can't help adding a little dig: "I do miss speeding on my Vespa though."

Officer Dick's eyes open wide, clearly fearful that Tommy will reveal more about his misdeeds. Instead, Tommy just grins and shakes his hand.

Captain McCoy interrupts this charming scene: "In addition to a ceremony in your honor, where you will receive an official commendation, the La Jolla Police Department would like to do something for you, Mr. Daniels."

Tommy pictures a hundred-dollar reward or maybe a chance to do a ride-along with a cop.

Captain McCoy continues, "We would like to buy you a new Vespa scooter to replace the one that was destroyed."

For the first time in days, Tommy feels genuinely joyful. Before he can celebrate, the man in the suit shakes Tommy's hand.

"Mr. Daniels, my name is Ardie Kapoor and I am the president of Swiftee Mart Corporation. I would like to thank you on behalf of everyone at our company for finally bringing our days of fear to an end. Now, our employees and customers are safe once again. Let me tell you, after seeing that footage, I wouldn't want to get in a fight with you!"

Tommy's parents and the three men laugh, as Tommy tries to absorb all the kind words that are coming his way. Mr. Kapoor reaches into his suit pocket and pulls out an envelope, handing it to Tommy.

"This is a token of our heartfelt and sincere appreciation."

Tommy excitedly opens the envelope to reveal a check. He has to examine the amount written on the check several times, because he can't believe it. It says, "$10,000"!

Tommy hugs Mr. Kapoor and the two cops. Then, he hugs his dad and mom while shouting for joy. Their long nightmare is finally over. He can help his parents with their money problems and he can pay for college.

And he gets his Vespa.

EPILOGUE

 *Soundtrack: General Public – "Tenderness"*

TOMMY DANIELS IS deep into his first semester of college and it's the last day before winter break. Leaving film class, he is very fashionable in his tailored suit and thin tie. Very Mod. Walking with him is Carl Ives, one of his new friends.

Carl explains, "Though it wasn't universally loved at the time of its release, *Vertigo* may be Hitchcock's most complex and complete work."

"The film's deconstruction of masculinity is especially profound," Tommy responds. "It was a masterwork to cast someone like Jimmy Stewart in the role of a repeatedly emasculated protagonist who simultaneously attempts to make a woman conform to his ideals of femininity."

Carl nods.

"Precisely. The mise-en-scène and cinematography are pretty extraordinary as well. The use of color and the utilization of real locations in Northern California are breathtaking."

Following some more geeky film discussions, Tommy says goodbye to Carl and heads over to a payphone. He drops in a quarter and calls his parents at work.

Both Frank and Rebecca Daniels are now employed at the Swiftee Mart in La Jolla. After receiving the check from Ardie Kapoor of the Swiftee Mart Corporation, Tommy told him about the difficulty his parents were having in finding jobs. A week later, his parents received a letter offering them both employment. Tommy's parents went through an intensive training program and now run the local Swiftee Mart together. Tommy's dad has finally let go of his obsession with public appearances. Rather than being ashamed about working at a convenience store and not being rich, he is proud that he and his wife have steady jobs and can support themselves. They have even moved into a more modest abode: a two-bedroom townhouse.

"Hey, Tommy!" Tommy's dad exclaims on the phone. "How did your exams go?"

"Not bad," Tommy responds. "I'm pretty sure I aced my film test. How's work?"

"Great! Business is up, we have nice customers, and I have the prettiest coworker ever."

Tommy hears his mom laugh in the background.

His dad adds, "We've had a pretty good few months, haven't we, Son?"

After his conversation with his dad, Tommy strolls through the quad with a smile on his face. Suddenly, Cassidy—she of the RV and the oily, crazy sex—jumps out of the bushes. Tommy nearly leaps out of his skin. Though startled, Tommy isn't too surprised to see her, since she's been following him around the last few weeks after somehow finding out where he goes to school. Tommy wonders if he yelled out his college plans during their sexual escapades. Heaven knows, they both screamed out a lot of weird shit.

Cassidy shouts, "Tommy, my love, why do you keep running from true love? I'll keep fighting for us! You're the best lay I've ever had!"

"Please, just leave me alone!"

Tommy hurries away before she can make much of a scene. Running through the bushes, he runs into a couple of guys.

"Hey, Tommy!" both men shout nearly in unison.

It's Jake and José, the two guys who gave Tommy a ride in the shitty-smelling pig and chicken truck on his adventures. They now work at Tommy's university. Sometimes, Tommy meets them for lunch and they all hang out together and share stories.

"Is that crazy woman following you around again?" Jake wonders.

Tommy nods.

Jose announces, "Don't worry, man, we'll run some interference for you!"

Tommy gives them high fives and feels lucky he has so many great friends.

"Thanks, guys! See you soon!"

Back on the main path, Tommy speeds along until he spots his former adversary, David W. Tush, across the quad. Old Tushy's life has taken a bit of left turn since Stephanie rejected him. He is now a bearded existentialist, who frequently hands out fliers and protests the ills of humanity. He is spending this afternoon giving a speech about some hippie cause. He has a hot bohemian chick next to him. Tommy laughs at how different David is and wonders what his new cohort would think if they saw photos of him from just six months earlier.

A group of cult members dance and sing in the quad. Tommy ponders if it is the same cult that tried its hardest to indoctrinate him. Not wanting to give them another chance, he increases his pace. Abruptly, one of the members—a young woman with a gloriously shaved head—runs up to Tommy. He tries to brush her away, but she gives him a hug. He regards her more closely and notices there's something familiar about her. Then, it hits him . . . it's Stephanie! She grabs a hold of his hands affectionately.

"Tommy, it is blissful to see you."

Tommy is dumbfounded, shocked to see his one-time love, especially with a shaved head and participating in a cult.

"What happened to you, Stephanie?"

"You did, Tommy."

She smiles broadly.

"After we broke up and I hurt you so much, I listened to that mixtape hundreds of times. I realized I never took the time to understand you or myself before. I sat down and reevaluated my life. Because of my upbringing, I had grown obsessed with material things."

"And now?"

"Now, I am different. I have reached enlightenment. I have given up material things and taken a vow of poverty. I think I finally understand you and your single-minded focus. Krishna is my Vespa."

They say their goodbyes and Tommy strolls away in a daze, trying to come to terms with the random encounter with his ex.

Tommy heads to a large lecture hall. On the door is a sign that reads, "Lecture by Dr. Harvey, Author of the New Children's Book *Victor the Vespa*." Tommy enters and stands at the back while Dr. Harvey lectures in front of a packed room about his inspirations and writing process. He is wearing a red cowboy hat with a miniature Vespa attached to the top. Dr. Harvey spots Tommy and tips his hat in his direction.

During the freewheeling, jovial question-and-answer section of the lecture, someone in the audience asks what Dr. Harvey's next book will be about. Dr. Harvey smiles.

He reveals, "My next book is going to be something rather different, my friend. It's going to be a novel rather than a children's book."

Someone shouts, "What's it about?"

"Thank you for asking so nicely, good sir. It's about a teenager's obsession with Mod culture and Vespas."

Another audience member yells, "Do you have a title yet?"

"Ah yes, the title. It will be called *The Scooter Chronicles.*"

Dr. Harvey winks at Tommy, who grins and gives him a thumbs up.

As Tommy walks out of the lecture hall, he takes a check out of his pocket. It's from Dr. Harvey for $2,000. Under the "Memo" section, it says, "Commission for groovy ideas."

Tommy walks to the parking lot. He pauses and smiles. There's his Vespa: a blue P200. On the seat sits a girl in a miniskirt and boots. Her face is concealed by the large camera she has pressed against her eye. She snaps several photos of Tommy, then lowers the camera. It's Emmy!

Tommy walks up to the girl of his dreams and kisses her. She broke up with Aston a while ago and succeeded in making it into art school. Though her dad had threatened to cut her off financially, it turned out he wasn't quite the hard ass he pretended to be. He respected Emmy's gumption and told her, in the end, he just wanted her to be happy.

Emmy and Tommy have been dating for a couple months and he feels like the luckiest guy in the world.

She hands him a framed photograph.

"What's this?" Tommy asks.

Emmy smiles as Tommy looks down at the frame. It's a photo of Tommy on his silver Vespa GS from the day they first met. Tommy studies the expression on his face in that moment: It's a mixture of elation, relief, and, as corny as it may sound, love.

Emmy beams, "This is the photo I used to win that contest I told you about. It was school wide! My professor says I should submit it to one of those scooter magazines you always have around, to see if I can get it published!"

"That's amazing!" Tommy exclaims.

He hugs her.

"So, are you up for that scooter rally tomorrow?"

She asks, "Have you met me before?"

They both laugh.

Tommy announces, "After that, I got a new job assignment."

"Ozzy?"

"Yeah, he wants me to help put together some footage for his big comeback. Plus, Jimmy will be there!"

"The king of the Mods? Excellent!"

Tommy adds, "I heard he has some more stories to tell me about his Mod days in London."

Tommy takes out his keys.

"You ready to ride?"

Emmy smiles. They kiss again. Tommy gets on his Vespa, Emmy's arms wrapped around him.

They ride away.

IT'S A WAY OF LIFE:
THE 1980S MOD REVIVAL IN SOUTHERN CALIFORNIA
by Bart Mendoza

> *Modism, Mod living, is an aphorism for clean living under difficult circumstances.*
>
> —Peter Alexander Edwin Meaden

READY STEADY GO

If you would have asked any Mod from the scene's original mid-1960s British heyday where the next revival of said youth subculture might take place, it's likely sunny Southern California would be the last location anyone thought of.

And yet starting around 1980, young Mods began to appear in large numbers around Los Angeles and San Diego, complete with clubs and zines catering to the new modernists. Subsequently, what became known simply as the "American Mod Revival" spread nationwide, with notable scenes in San Francisco, Chicago, and New Jersey. Quickly interlocked with the purist Mod scene were the burgeoning ska revival groups and the garage/psychedelic aficionados—a.k.a., the Paisley Underground—all of which originally drew largely from the same audiences.

As much as Mod is about the cool clothes and the sharp rides, music is at its core. Following on from the original sixties-era U.K. Mod explosion, there had already been a revival in England during the late seventies, led by bands such as the Jam, the Chords, and the Purple Hearts, all retaining key influences while adding a punk edge.

Fast forward a few years and the early 1980s saw "Mod" become a buzz word in America. Why did it happen? Certainly the release of the film *Quadrophenia* in 1979 was a big part of it, as were the visits stateside from groups such as Secret Affair to venues like Whiskey a Go Go (August 12, 1980). The U.S. was also coming out of the skinny tie, power-pop era with bands like the Plimsouls, the Knack, and 20/20 roaming the clubs of the day, all with Mod influences. There was even a great R&B combo, of natural appeal to Mods, already performing: the Crawdaddys. But it was the emergence of a string of great, if largely unsung, bands that kicked things over the edge in that pre-MTV era. It was a time when going out and hearing live music was the social event of choice for anyone under thirty and combos such as the Untouchables, the Question, Manual Scan, and the Patterns were gigging constantly to growing and enthusiastic crowds.

With all this going on, it was only natural that a few kids and young adults would be influenced. But it became something much more than that: a large community emerged, traces of which still remain today.

PARTY AT GROUND ZERO

Of course Mod isn't a one-size-fits-all thing. It's definitely a lifestyle. The outline is there, but there are many ways in which it's an individual thing as well, including musical taste. Your preference can be rocksteady or power pop or something else.

I perhaps have a unique perspective on Mod in the U.S. having been a Mod since 1978, a member of the band Manual Scan, the publisher of the Modzine *Sound Affects*, a reporter for many publications and zines, and the promoter of many Mod events, including the New Sounds Music Festival. Never even had an automobile driver's license. Vespa all the way.

I was part of a small group of kids/young adults who were already embracing the Mod lifestyle when director Frank Roddam decided to make the movie *Quadrophenia*, based on the Who's 1973 album with the same name. The release of the film in 1979 changed things. The existing Mods in the area, of course, embraced it, some of them attending preview screenings. But for the public at large in the U.S. it was the first real look at "Mod" and it struck a chord with many. Having attended an advance showing of the film, I can vouch for the feeling of exhilaration after seeing it for the first time; it's a powerful film. For decades since, a screening of *Quadrophenia* at a local art house has been excuse enough to get a few dozen scooters out for a ride, with people quoting the onscreen action.

Coincidentally, the publication that same year of the book *Mods!* by Richard Barnes, filled with photos and memorabilia from the original sixties Mods, gave many the perfect template for the look and attitude of the original crews and was referred to by many as the scene's "bible."

If things could be pinpointed down to a flashpoint, where the American Mod movement could be seen to gain focus, it's likely the creation of two venues: Los Angeles's O.N. Klub at the start of 1982 and San Diego's Kings Road Cafe soon after. There had been events before with Mod appeal and plenty of house parties, but these two locations showed there was a large enough audience to sustain a movement . . . which of course led to more shows.

The Kings Road Cafe (previously called the International Blend) was run by Peter Verbugge, who was also a DJ and music promoter. Originally run by Ruben Seja, the venue was a coffee house with world, acoustic, and jazz music. When the first two Tuesday night Mod shows drew packed houses, as did a show by ska heroes the Equators, more and more events were added, with the name change in 1982 a clear indicator of its status in the music scene. During this time frame, Verbugge—who would go on to run major venues in San Diego and Seattle—also served as manager of the Crawdaddys and Manual Scan, giving him a unique perspective on the young scene.

Make no mistake: This was a youth movement, with most in their early twenties and younger. The Kings Road Cafe even had weekly 3 p.m. teen dances for the school-age kids. Many high schools during this time frame also hosted regular Friday night dances that often featured Mod bands.

In a way, the Kings Road Cafe brought together both past and present elements of Mod music, as virtual house band Manual Scan played original material while sixties-inspired groups like the Hedgehogs—with several members fresh out of high school and soon to splinter into such combos as the Tell Tale Hearst, thee Nashville Ramblers, and the revised Crawdaddys—concentrated on recreating a particular vintage sound to go with their look, which in their case was Hamburg-era Beatles. When local publications including *The Reader* wanted to do articles on the new scene, the Kings Road Cafe was the obvious place to go, with Manual Scan amongst those called in to pose around a Vespa brought in and placed on the small club's stage.

It's important to note how important the local media's support in both Los Angeles and San Diego was to the growth of the Mod scene. In the pre-internet days, zines were crucial for spreading the word about music and various events. There were numerous such publications during this time frame devoted to Mod, including *Topped Up*, *Sound Affects*, and *Getting Started*. Most of them were true DIY wonders in all their Xerox glory, but there were more professional endeavors as well, the best of which was Los Angeles-based *Twist Magazine*. Lasting several issues, its publisher David Lumian also managed the Untouchables at the time, later going on to work with punk band the Descendants and Paisley Underground band the Dream Syndicate. Other zines worth checking out included San Francisco's *Whaaam!*, with copies available at places like Tower Records, and *Ready*

Steady Read, an early nineties mag. Despite being Northern California-based, both zines had significant audiences in Southern California.

Interestingly, two U.K. publications also had an important impact on the U.S. Mod revival. *The Phoenix List* was a biweekly publication that ran roughly from 1983 to 1988, listing all Mod events and news. Really just a couple of folded over pages of tightly packed, Xeroxed info, its importance in getting the word out about shows or music cannot be understated. At first, the focus was on London in particular and England in general, but before too long international coverage was included, with regular reports from Los Angeles and San Diego. While other U.K. and European Modzines included some foreign reporting, *The Phoenix List* became one of the two main conduits of info between the American and British Mod scenes. The publication eventually spun off a label, Unicorn Records, which for a few years released records by what they dubbed "Phase III Bands," following on from the original sixties Mod scene and the late seventies revival. The eighties Phase III groups included the American Mod bands, such as the Key, Manual Scan, and ska combo the Donkey Show.

The other major info source was *In the Crowd*. Published by Derek Shepherd, there were 30 issues released between 1983 and 1990, as it went from stapled, photocopied pages to professional, glossy ones. A couple of issues even had flexi discs. No other publication had the same thorough coverage of the worldwide scene. Despite being a British publication, it would often have pages of info on American happenings. Shepard continued reporting on Mod between 1990 and 1998 with a subsequent publication, *Tailor Made*, which ran for nine issues.

These publications were largely preaching to the converted. What brought Mod culture to teens in the outlying suburbs was the support of local media. One needed only look at the coverage of Mod events on local news and talk shows of the day to see the immediate appeal of the scene: young and fresh devotees who look forward with an eye on the past, all while wearing stylish clothes and zipping around on scooters. It's photogenic. Though the on-camera reporters and announcers often got the details wrong, for a lot of kids those TV stories and newspaper articles were a big draw. The further away you were from the center of things, the more the camaraderie of the Mod community likely appealed.

On the sounds side, at first young Mods listened to the records coming out of England, in addition to sixties music. But pretty soon the area's local combos began to issue their own singles and EPs. They were all relatively small pressings, usually under 1,000 copies, but at the time it was much rarer for performers to release music. There was support for the groups and their records from their fans and college radio, as well as from occasional coverage in press and radio programs such as *Rodney on the ROQ* on the highly influential station KROQ-FM.

In this instant access world we live in today, it's easy to forget just how difficult it was in the early 1980s to come across records and music magazines. Cable TV was still new and not widely available, so record stores, radio, and press were the only games in town in terms of exposing people to music. Record stores, in particular, were plentiful with chain record stores everywhere, but not every neighborhood had a store that carried "imports." And even then, ones that did really only carried the bigger names; so, while you might find a Secret Affair single, good luck with Back to Zero.

Record stores were the hub of musical activity, haunted by music fans/Mods every opportunity they could get. It was a place to learn about new tunes and artists, drop off or pick up the latest gig flyers, and, more than anything, meet like-minded folks. Two major components of San Diego's Mod community, from the La Jolla and

East County neighborhoods, actually met for the first time in 1981 in the singles section of the Sports Arena Tower Records.

Though only separated by 112 miles, there were significant differences in music between San Diego and Los Angeles. Initially, Los Angeles had a more power pop and ska sound and featured a lot of trios, such as the Key and Chardon Square. Meanwhile, San Diego featured a much heavier dose of British R&B, jangly garage, and sixties psyche in their mix, as shown by groups like the Event. There were also a lot of sixties-influenced bands in San Diego, such as garage rockers the Tell-Tale Hearts, who might not have declared themselves as Mod, but were popular with those who did.

Today, Mod-themed DJ events are fairly common, but during this time period it was the bands that drew all the attention, with house parties a big focus. Often, someone was spinning discs, but during the eighties there was almost always a band or two present. There were a few spots that had regular Mod nights, such as the Lhasa Club in Los Angeles, which featured DJ Bryan Fox.

Most of the key bands of the day released at least a single, including the Question, the Jetz, Manual Scan, and the Commoners. There are a few compilation albums out there that feature a few bands from the era's U.S. Mod scene, including *This Is Mod Volume 6 – The U.S. of Mod* (Cherry Red / Anagram, 1997) and the box set *Millions Like Us* (Cherry Red, 2015), both CD only. To date the only compilation to focus mainly on Southern California is a vinyl bootleg, *Idealistic Youth Volume 1: California*, which features 11 bands, only one of which is not from Southern California (Start, a Bay Area trio).

The biggest draw during this time was easily ska combo the Untouchables. Formed in 1981, by late 1982 they had become the house band of the Los Angeles Roxy. They scored a memorable cameo in the 1984 cult classic movie *Repo Man* and went on to become the only band of the original movement to score any chart activity, with two U.K. singles in 1985: "Free Yourself" (#26) and "I Spy For The F.B.I." (#59 and produced by Jerry Dammers of the Specials, on Stiff Records no less).

There was crossover between the bands as well, not just with LA bands in SD and vice versa but on the collaborative front as well. Admittedly, there were band rivalries, with which fans could sometimes get carried away. When one scene band got a plum gig opening for a major touring ska band, the fans of another band, who felt *they* should be on the bill, let the air out of their tires at the venue. Prankish behavior for the most part.

Still, for the most part, it was a tight knit community. When Manual Scan was about to cancel a show at the Concert Factory in Orange County because their bassist couldn't make it, Carl Rusk of the Hedgehogs stepped in and played the concert. The title track to the Untouchables debut album, *Wild Child* (U.K.#51, 1985), was a co-write between the band's guitarist, Clyde Grimes, and the Question's front man, Tony Rugalo.

These groups' concerts weren't just shows. They were events, at times almost like gospel revival shows in feel, complete with fervent crowds. As much as a Jam show was about the music, it was also a chance to meet up with friends and like-minded kids, maybe fall in love, and definitely have a good time. It wasn't unusual to meet Mods from other countries at these shows drawn by the same forces. Paul Weller, now the "Modfather," continues to draw reverent crowds, but nothing will ever match the reactions of those lucky Jam fans that got to see the original trio in action.

SATURDAY'S KIDS

The Los Angeles and San Diego scenes had much in common, but where the City of Angels had the clear advantage was in shopping and ground zero in the day was Melrose Avenue. It's hard to imagine now, when even the parking is restricted on the street, but once it was the home of numerous hip used and new clothing stores, such as Aardvark's, Poseur, and Flip! During the early part of the Mod scene it would not be uncommon to see dozens of scooters parked along Melrose, exploring the area's sartorial splendor. It also didn't hurt that there were numerous record stores there, including Aron's, Vinyl Fetish, and Rene's.

In terms of clothes, there were some basic differences between U.K. Mods and U.S. Mods. Parkas in England are a necessity in the cold, damp, drizzly weather. In America, it was more of a symbolic fashion statement. The warm weather and bulkiness prevented them from becoming more common.

A guy's clothing was pretty basic: a narrow lapel, three-button jacket, button-down or (preferably) tab-collar shirt, skinny tie, pegged pants and, for your feet, either desert boots, loafers, or Chelsea boots. Since they were worn by Paul Weller, bowling shoes were also popular for a while, to the great consternation of area bowling alleys. As for the ladies, while there were a few who went for the classic U.K. Mod girl look, in the U.S. it was a more general sixties look, with cocktail dresses and suits the norm, as you might have seen on many mid-1960s TV sitcoms' teen dance sequences.

At the time, thrift store picking was in its early stages, so there were many used treasures to be found cheap; but there were also numerous clothing distributors that had original stock available from decades past. One in San Diego, Ellis & Co, even had the clothes separated out by year. Nothing more authentic then heading straight to "1965" and suiting up. That well dried up when overseas merchants began buying out the entire stock of some places, a fate that befell a local record shop as well.

One advantage that San Diego did have was its proximity to Mexico. A bit of investigation sometimes turned up some old stock and everyone headed there for their Beatles boots for a while; bands such as Mod Fun stocked up on inexpensive Fred Perry's and op-art shirts. It also didn't hurt that Mexico's drinking age was 18 (no one carded anyway!) and all the bars and boutiques along Tijuana's infamous Revolucion Avenue were open 24 hours. Today, you have to have a passport to cross the border, but you could just walk across then. It was a rite of passage for many generations of Southern Californians and a party from the moment you got there.

Most of the clubs had DJs, but occasionally there was live music, such as a show in 1984 with the Untouchables, Manual Scan, and soul combo the Big Express at Rancho Grande, a block-long bar that was on the second floor of a building. Today, there is a thriving Mod scene in Tijuana, but at the time the audience was mostly comprised of young Americans, many in various stages of intoxication. There was minimal crowd control at events back then and it was possible you might get hurt. It's the sort of situation that could never happen today. When Big Express took the stage, the crowd—including Mods from as far away as San Francisco—surged forward and jammed up against the stage. By the time Manual Scan was on, police had arrived and the band had to stop playing, as people up front were pulled out of the crowd. The free-standing "stage" had been pushed slowly back by the audience, who despite being packed in like sardines, remained enthusiastic. The Untouchables almost didn't get to play, but it was feared the situation would become worse if they didn't, so the show went on, under the watchful eye of the authorities. The bar's manager was thrilled with the over-capacity crowd that night and spoke of having the bands back as soon as possible, but he never did.

GOING MOBILE

Scooters, specifically vintage metal vehicles such as Vespas and Lambrettas, were a status symbol of the Mod revival. Both men and women drove them, with clubs forming almost immediately. There are many reasons for owning a scooter, but probably the best is simply the feeling of driving it. A Vespa ride has been described as like being on a worldwide theme park ride and, while your mileage may vary, there is no denying that it can be a lot of fun. A scooter zipping around often draws attention; little kids in particular love them.

But when you get a whole bunch of them together? That will bring people out of the shops to watch. You can see it in their eyes. As a procession of scooters winds its way around to someplace, the reactions from other drivers and pedestrians is noticeable. There are definitely a few grumps in the mix, obviously wondering if all the scooters in traffic will make them late for something, but in the rest, there is a clear fascination. There is a distinct appeal to these machines. Being at the wheel of a car can feel like a chore, but this is different.

Scooters have a long history in Southern California. There have been shops in the area that stocked them since the early sixties and manufacturers such as Honda have had scooters in their product lines and showrooms for decades. To be honest, at that particular point in history, at least in the States, scooters were really often considered mostly for older folks. Indeed, that's where many would find their first scooters.

The first large wave of interest in scooters among American youth came in the late seventies as part of the original Mod revival. The vehicles owners then were largely fans of sixties rock, soul, and ska, and scooters were the transportation of choice to the many concerts and dances sponsored by the various local scooter clubs. At the peak of the eighties Mod revival, one of the bigger scooter rallies might have over 150 scooters and it was pretty common to see 40 or more scooters for just a screening of the movie *Dance Craze*.

Later on, beautifying your ride using imported parts, chroming, or other methods became de rigueur, but early on, just having a running scooter was enough, with no shame in a bit of rust or in a less-than-perfect scoot. One San Diego Mod even had front crash bars crafted from the legs of an old school chair attached to his Lambretta. It looked pretty good! There were a few scoots that went for having a lot of lights, but that fad died out quickly due to the difficulty of maintaining the electrical system amidst the salt air of the coast. For a while, people would attach stuffed animals to their backrests, facing the driver behind the scooter. I have memories of seeing Wile E. Coyote, the Pink Panther, and Yosemite Sam cruising down the 5 Freeway on the back of Vespas headed to rallies.

Another part of the initial appeal was the hunt. People had scooters lying in garages undriven, so it was still possible to find a used one for a few hundred dollars. They were even occasionally found at yard sales.

Lots of scooter clubs existed in those days, such as the 100 Faces (which included Scott Chain of Orange County Vespa retail powerhouse Scooterville) and the Coronado-based group the Dancing Skeletons, with many of them hosting occasional reunions in subsequent years. San Diego's Secret Society is still going strong! Formed in 1983 by a ragtag bunch of scooterists and Mods who gathered on Sunday nights at Hillcrest's taco shop La Posta, it is a solid representation of the type of kids that were involved in the early Mod revival scene. Members would go on to become teachers, police officers, writers, and so on, with the club becoming part of San Diego's cultural fabric not just through rallies, poker runs, and picnics, but also through their support of the New Sounds Music Festival, Sound Affects fanzine, and numerous concerts. Without their assistance, performers such as New Jersey's Mod Fun, Boys About Town, and a one-off group formed especially for the New Sounds show of 1986—featuring members of the Times, the Jetset, the Merton Parkas, and Manual Scan—would never have played in the area.

Perhaps the highpoint of the scooter scene was in 1984 when members of both the 100 Faces and Secret Society clubs were seen riding their scooters in the video by the Three O'Clock for their song "Jet Fighter Man."

Within a few years Mods at scooter rallies became the minority as "scooter boys," with a general jean and t-shirt look—mixed with some camouflage—took over and racing/cutdown scooters became the focus. Ska and soul became (and continues to be) the dominant music for the scooter scene.

THE JAM

The first peak of the original Southern California Mod scene would be the Jam's Perkins Palace appearances on May 29-31, 1982.

They had been to Los Angeles before: Weller and company had been annual visitors between 1977 and 1980, which of course had brought out all the suited fans. But 1982 was different. The Jam skipped the West Coast in 1981, in fact performing only one concert in the U.S. that year—May 26 at the Ritz in New York, a warm up to their appearance the next night on NBC's Tom Snyder-hosted *Tomorrow* program.

This three-night stand/residency showed just how big the Mod community had grown in that one-year absence. Three sold out nights.

To be clear, audiences were mixed, with frat boys and record company types rubbing elbows with Mods who came from throughout the Southland, including en masse from San Diego. Nevertheless, the throng of scooters parked on the street showed who the largest group of fans was. The shows were a big deal and the *Los Angeles Times* published an extensive review of the shows, with San Diego Mods Dean Curtis and Larry Nadler pictured.

While there had been much cross-pollination between Los Angeles and San Diego in the preceding year, this was the first time such a huge number of Mods from the two areas comingled, as they filled area hotels and had a 72-hour Mod party.

Picking up folks along the way, the group I was a part of took the scenic route—Highway 101 up the coast. Looking back, we were all young and full of energy, not to mention optimism and adrenaline in anticipation of seeing our musical heroes. So, the long ride went by in a blur, with our group of scooters drawing attention from civilians along the way. Everybody, except those driving behind them, loves scooter rallies.

Running on adrenaline, we met up with other friends and took over a Pasadena motel. We were fortunate enough that it was run by a gentleman who didn't mind having scooters driving in and out all night and rooms full of boisterous kids blasting music. Apparently not all area motel owners were as understanding, as quite a few friends ended up crashing with our San Diego contingent after being kicked out of their abodes for general rowdiness.

The Jam played a blinding 18-song set, mingling with their audience both at sound checks and after the show. It was rumored that our motel owner even bought a scalped ticket and attended the concert to see what the fuss was all about.

MOD MOMENTS:
IMAGES FROM THE 1980S SOUTHERN CALIFORNIA MOD REVIVAL

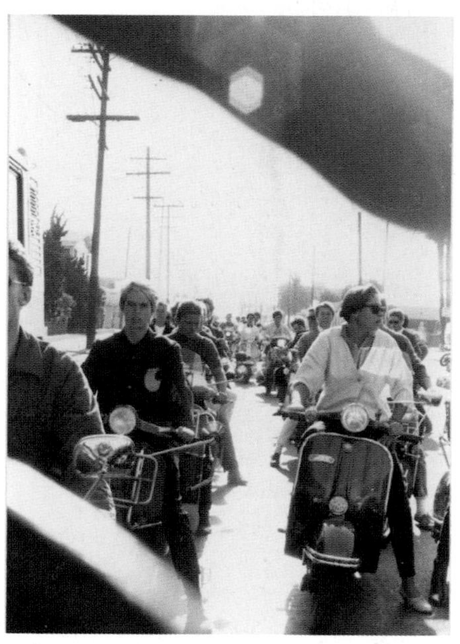

April 1985. *From the collection of Bart Mendoza.*

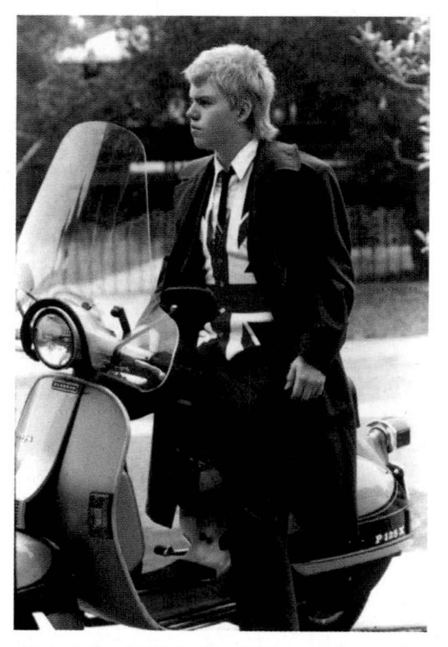

Kevin Ring, guitarist for Manual Scan and other bands, with his first scooter, circa 1981. *Photo by Anne Ring.*

From the collection of Bart Mendoza.

Mod rally in Fullerton, CA. *From the collection of Bart Mendoza.*

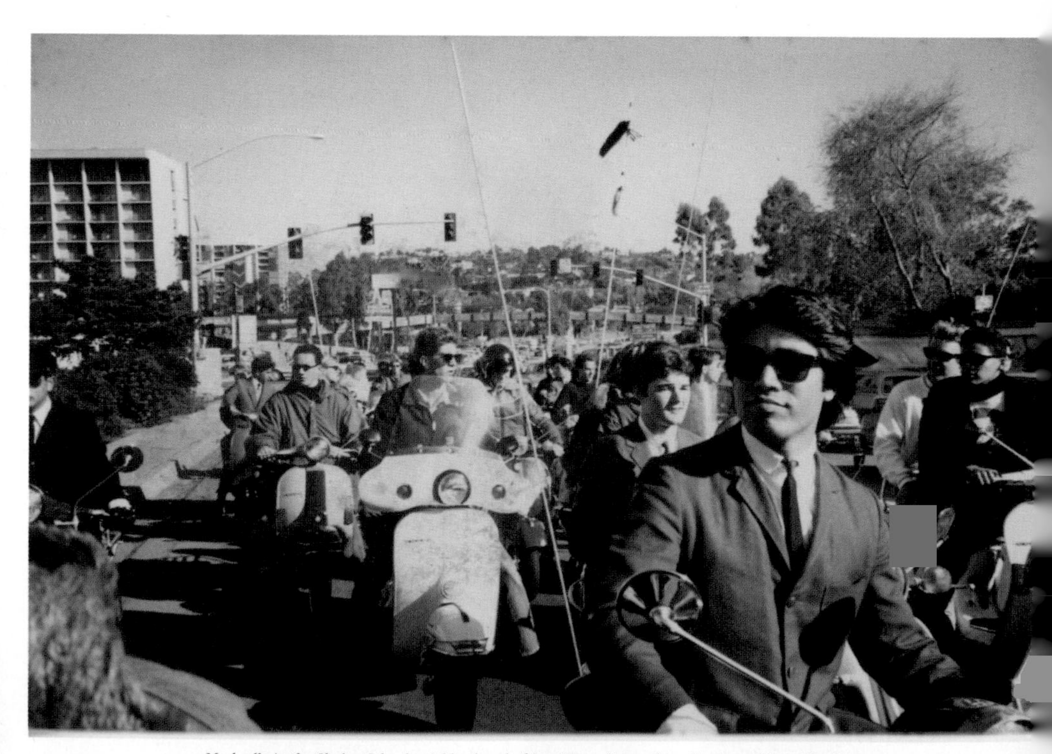

Mod rally in the Shelter Island neighborhood of San Diego. *From the collection of Bart Mendoza.*

The Nashville Ramblers at the Cavern Club on November 30, 1986. *From the collection of Bart Mendoza.*

The Key at JP's Nightclub in Point Loma, San Diego. *From the collection of Bart Mendoza.*

Roddy Bogawa of the Odds. *From the collection of Roddy Bogawa.*

The Three O'Clock. *From the collection of Roddy Bogawa.*

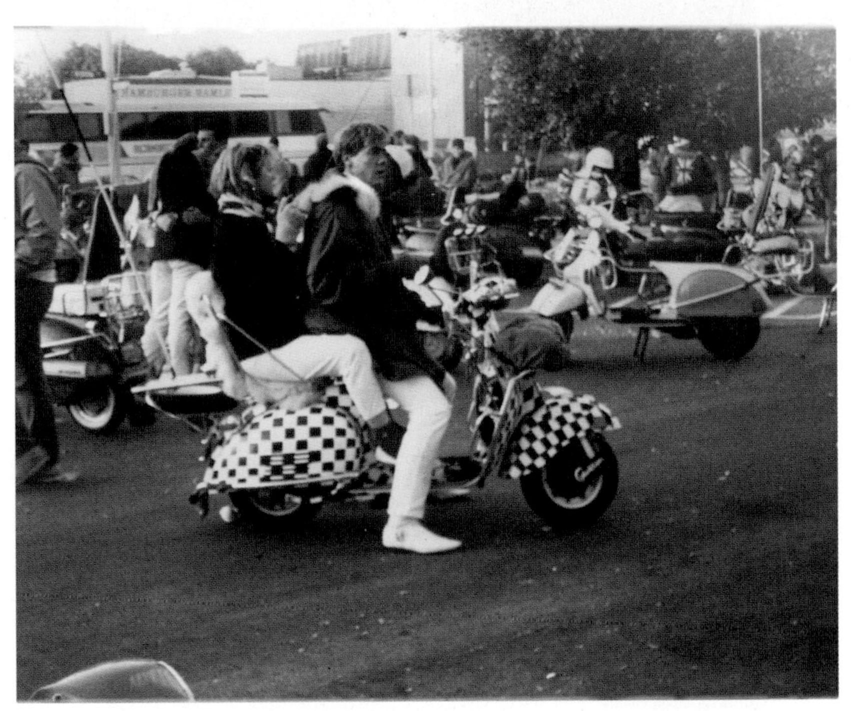

Mod rally in Los Angeles in January 1985. *From the collection of Bart Mendoza.*

January 1985. *From the collection of Bart Mendoza.*

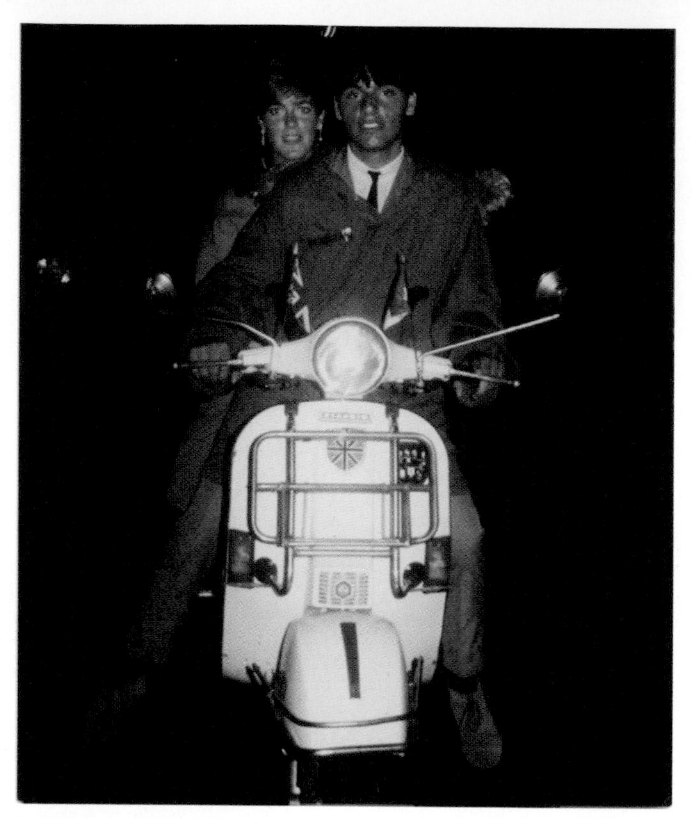

Joe Mendoza and friend at Club Zu on August 29, 1984. *From the collection of Bart Mendoza.*

Melrose Avenue in June 1982. *From the collection of Bart Mendoza.*

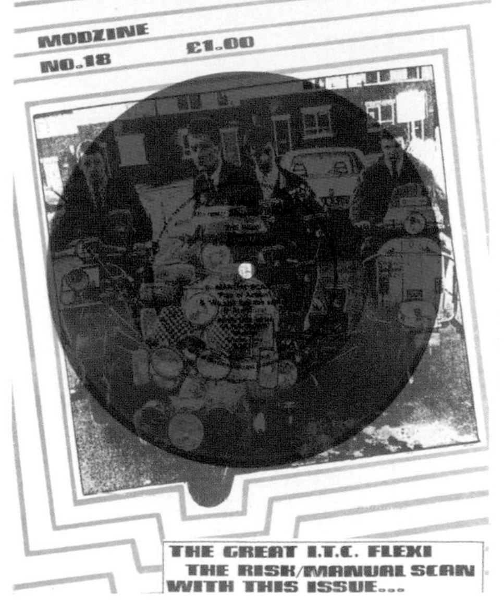

From the collection of Bart Mendoza.

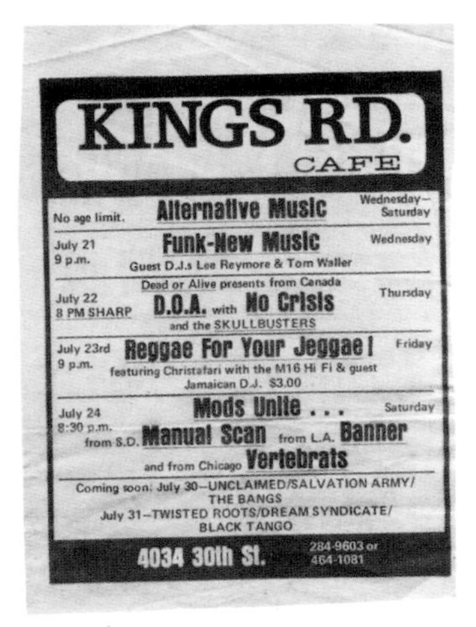

From the collection of Bart Mendoza.

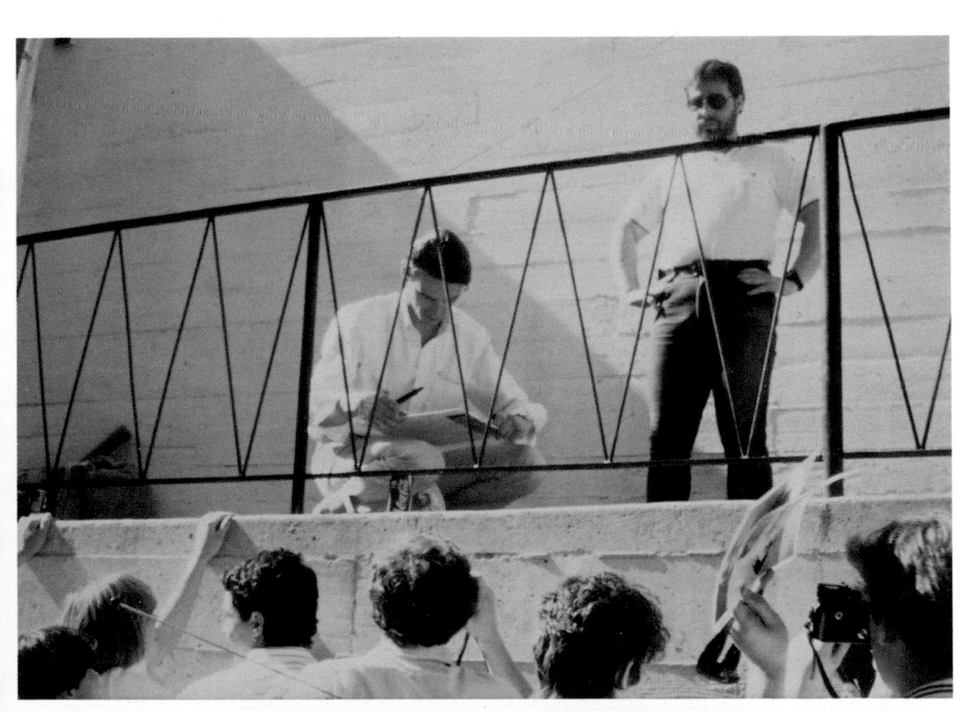

Paul Weller. *From the collection of Roddy Bogawa.*

COVER FOR DR. HARVEY'S *VICTOR THE VESPA*

by Ralph Cosentino

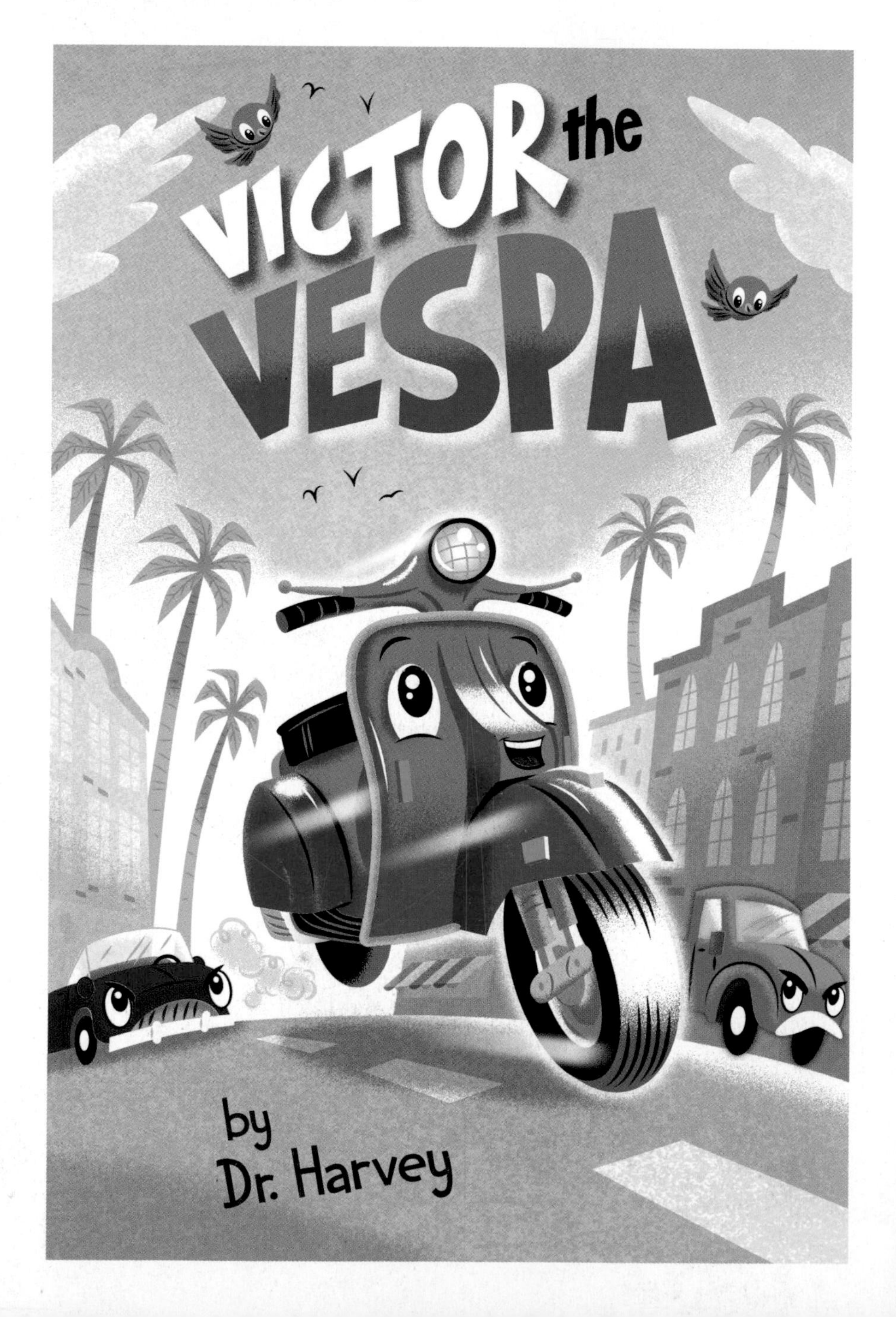

The next Paul Weller performance in Los Angeles would be with the Style Council, his Mod/punk/power pop hybrid that had a more soulful sound. Many Mods followed his lead.

WHAT'S SHE DONE TO YOUR MIND?

By 1983, many of the originals in Los Angeles began to move on. While the early Southern California Mod scene took much of its imagery from the mid-1960s, the newly minted Paisley Underground added later influences as well, so things opened up a bit in term of both look and sound. Fashion, in particular, spanned from the Beatles Revolver/Rubber Soul casual cool to the Jam's black-and-white suits.

The phrase "Paisley Underground" was coined by Michael Quercio to describe a concert bill that included his band the Three O'Clock, as well as the Bangles and the Rain Parade. Davis, CA was a key location in the formation of the scene, while San Diego missed out on the psychedelic sounds except for visiting bands, such as Bang and the pre-Three O'Clock combo the Salvation Army, both of whom had Manual Scan open for them at the Kings Road Cafe.

While the Paisley Underground had many things in common with the Mod scene, the biggest difference was in the level of success the bands experienced. All of the key bands associated with the scene landed major label deals and experienced significant chart action and/or airplay, particularly the Bangles who scored platinum album sales and scored eight top 40 hits, including two #1's: "Walk Like an Egyptian" (1986) and "Eternal Flame" (1989). Even lesser known bands such as Eyes of Mind, featuring Michael Quercio's former Salvation Army bandmate Troy Howell, scored deals with major indies, such as Bomp Records subsidiary Voxx Records.

By 1985, there were still plenty of shows happening in San Diego. The Kings Road Cafe faded away, but Headquarters in the Pacific

Beach neighborhood continued on for a year or so. With many of the originals now over 21, most of their shows started to take place at regular clubs with alcohol. Roots rock, as exemplified by the Beat Farmers and the Paladins, took hold. This blend of sixties folk and garage rock was the sounds of choice for many, with bands such as the Tell-Tale Hearts—featuring former members of the Kings Road favorites the Hedgehogs—and the Gravedigger V playing out. There was still a sizeable population of Mods, but there wouldn't be another Mod-oriented venue in San Diego again until 2581 opened up in the North Park neighborhood circa 1988, lasting about two years.

Around the same time, sixties music fans in Los Angeles had the Cavern Club open in April 1985, run by Bomp Records head honcho Greg Shaw. It quickly became the center of the Mod universe in Southern California, even chronicled in *People* magazine. The venue hosted its share of psychedelic, garage, and Mod bands from around the world, though it was mostly local combos. With an entrance located in an alley, it was a decidedly low-rent location and perfect for rock 'n' roll, though the lack of security—not a good thing anywhere, but especially in a dodgy area of Hollywood—meant there was occasional violence outside, which would sometimes creep inside. One infamous show featuring Mod Fun and U.K. trio the Risk ended with skinheads throwing chairs on the dance floor and attempting mayhem in the parking lot. Totally worth the risk for a young music fan.

NEW SOUNDS

There were several things that kept the focus of Mod on Southern California. A significant role was played by the generally good weather of the region. There's no way to understate the importance of being able to stage outdoor events and concerts—and scooter rallies—pretty much any weekend year-round, in contrast to other Mod scenes in climates with actual winters. It's part of what makes the area a major tourist destination as well.

But the biggest factor in bringing Mods to the area may have been San Diego's New Sounds Music Festival. Created to focus on sixties-influenced bands and Mod culture, the event started as a four-band bill topped by Mod Fun at the Encinitas all-ages venue Club Zu. By the next year, it was a major event complimented by other activities, ranging from scooter rallies to FM radio specials. These extra happenings meant that many performers scheduled extended stays in the area, with groups such as the Channel Islands trio the Risk, Arizona psychedelic rockers the Marshmallow Overcoat, and Squire frontman Anthony Meynell all making lengthy visits to San Diego.

Helmed by myself and, at first, Ron Friedman, and, later, Matt Fidelibus, there were seven New Sounds festivals from 1985 to 1991. I had been bringing groups to town for a while anyway, so the idea of focusing efforts appealed to me. The chance to do these events to benefit SDSU's student-run radio station KCR was even better. The motive for the New Sounds festivals was simply to promote and showcase music influenced by Mod/Sixties/Garage, in particular local groups like the Tell-Tale Hearts, the Nashville Ramblers, Donkey Show, the Trebels, and the Event. With short sets and a backline, it sometimes felt like a really, really cool jukebox. We were also lucky to have major support from the San Diego Union Tribune and 91X FM. Perhaps overambitious at times, these shows were a lot of work and filled with headaches, but they were mostly a lot of fun, a true labor of love.

By 1991, the scene had changed and amidst serious day-of-show turmoil, I decided the time had come to end the series of festivals. It was a spur-of-the-moment decision, caught by Mike Moon's camera on the day: You see me walk over to bassist Mark Zadarnowski and add the Kinks song "Where Have All the Good Times Gone" to the setlist . . . an appropriate addition, I felt, given the moment. My mid-song, stage left, greeting to someone off screen, is to SOMA owner (and Kinks fan) Len Paul.

There were many other attempts to stage large Mod events—including a Mod Rally circa 1988 at the Scottish Rite Temple in San Diego and a Mods May Day event at the John Anson Ford Theatre in Hollywood in 1989—but New Sounds was the only annual event. High points were many, including appearances by the Leopards, Anthony Meynell, and Jeff Connolly of the Lyres. The low point was definitely 1987 when the concert was shut down by the police while in progress. The following story might give some indication of just how "skin of our teeth" early events were and how the camaraderie in the scene transformed even less-than-positive adventures into memories you'd never want to forget.

Although we had filled out all relevant paperwork and paid all fees for the show, held at the now-defunct Palisade Garden's Skating Rink, we made sure to have several pre-meetings with the building's manager. After all, this location was almost too good to be true. It was centrally located in the North Park neighborhood and just about perfect for our kind of show. It featured a large parking lot for scooters, a wood dance floor/rink with a stage, and—best of all—a second level balcony that went all the way around the building . . . perfect for vendors.

With a bill scheduled to include No Doubt, the Rumble, and the Pandoras, the sheer amount of people that showed up on the day brought us to police attention. Various scooterists revving engines and weaving through traffic didn't help either. Police came around three times about noise and crowds in the street, but were overall friendly enough in dealing with myself and the building's owner. On the way out, one officer said, "You've got all your permits in order, right?" and the manager responded, "Yes," waving a piece of paper. All seemed okay as the officer walked about 100 feet away. But, then, all of a sudden he turned and shouted, "Let me see that!" The show unraveled at that point. Unfortunately, it turned out the manager of the building didn't want to spend cash on permits and so had just been waving a random utility bill. The sergeant was not amused and the show was ordered shut down on the spot. I had the fun task of walking on stage while a band was performing to tell the growing crowds it was over, barely two hours in.

Things actually got a little worse. My girlfriend at the time tried to get to the box office to refund ticket money, but it was too late. The manager took off with the receipts. It was the last we ever heard of him in a situation that made the local papers. "New Sounds" had become "No Sounds."

That was a down moment. Down but not out, as many people congregated at Presidio Park and before long a house was offered up, no parents included. While now a much smaller gathering, it was at least a place for out of towners to gather. The one plus to the early show stoppage was that we were able to reach some of the Los Angeles bands before they headed down to San Diego. Meanwhile, a fashion show took place on the stairs next to the kitchen and bands played in the living room and outdoors by the swimming pool. An epic party night that showed how everyone was happy to pitch in to make something happen.

We moved the event the following year to San Diego State University's 1,000 capacity Montezuma Hall and ran into problems on the day of the event once again. Campus security feared we were an all-day hardcore punk event and, on the morning of the show, threatened to cancel us. In the end, they greatly curtailed our hours, meaning bands had to trim their set times . . . something that didn't go over great with either fans or bands. In addition, some musicians objected to using a backline drum set, a necessity when you have so many groups performing. Somehow it all worked out well enough, with various members of campus security dancing at the side of the stage to the music of the festival's closer, ska favorite Donkey Show. That night, they offered us the venue for the following year.

The SDSU shows were probably the peak, with various members of the Bangles, Roger Manning of Jellyfish, and even Smiths guitarist Johnny Marr attending, but building renovations meant the last of the first run of New Sounds Music Festivals took place at SOMA.

I continued to bring groups to town after the run ended and promoted one more New Sounds fest in 1998, though with a wider pop range in booking and more of an international flavor.

Later, but equally vital to keeping the Mod fires burning, was Domenic Priore's cable TV program *It's Happening*, which featured live performances from bands like the Driving Wheels and the Nashville Ramblers. Bringing things closer to the modern era, former Tell-Tale Hearts bassist and future Ugly Things publisher Mike Stax would go on to run his own Mod night spot, *Hipsters*, at the turn of the century.

BLOOD AND ROSES

As you can imagine, the Mod revival wasn't always met with open arms. It was a time of teen tribes, so violence at night clubs and surrounding areas was a real possibility. With alternative music communities at the time being so small, much of the time there might be tension, especially since punks, rockabillies, and Mods often came out of the same group of school friends. Sometimes, things could be brutal, not just due to expected rival groups, but also from the basic surfer/frat dude/bro who might take drunken offense to seeing someone in a suit or on a Vespa at a club or even on the street. Things could be as random as simple verbal abuse from passing motorists or people throwing chunks of firewood at scooterists on a freeway. For some reason, kids wearing suits and ties or a paisley shirt brought out the worst in some and you could get jumped walking down the street or attending a show.

There was certainly animosity between some skinheads and Mods (or anyone on a scooter). In San Diego, a scooter club was threatened by a gang of skins who had been harassing area residents. They had recently taken to chasing scooterists in their cars/vans and promised to show up for a fight at the club's meeting place. It wasn't long before word got out to the greater music scene. Perhaps the wise thing to do would have been to cancel that week's meeting, but that didn't seem right. So, everyone drove to the meeting spot. For the first time in weeks, no club members were going to be absent. Pulling into the parking lot of the meeting spot, the scooter club was surprised to see dozens of other Mods, punks, and even a few rockabillies already there and partying. Fed up with harassment in general, many had come to support the scooter club. If it went down, they'd be there. If not, it'd be a parking lot party. Sure enough, a van full of skins came screeching up ready to do battle. When they saw the waiting crowd, they reversed out ASAP.

There was never any reason for this sort of thing, just testosterone, alcohol, and mob mentality. But the general public at times was no better, with the hesher crowd sometimes considering the wearing of a suit to be some sort of personal affront. In these modern, more enlightened times it might be hard to believe that a suit would cause such problems, but this wasn't just clothes we wore and music that we listened to; it was part and parcel of a lifestyle. Many of us wanted to defend our way of life, whether or not anyone was actually threatening it.

In the day, the authorities were often less than enthusiastic about Mods. Today, it all seems so harmless, but at the time there were issues with the police, who often confused the kids for punks and sometimes considered the movement as a whole to be a sort of gang. Basically, to many officers at the time, kids/young adults were trouble so police could be counted on to break up parties, ticket rallies, and harass people at shows . . . the usual wet blanket stuff. Things are different today, helped by the fact that several Mods eventually went into law enforcement.

THE KIDS ARE ALRIGHT

Much has changed in the world since the American Mod revival of the early 1980s, but Mod continues on, locally and internationally. The look is now considered classic cool. It will never go out of style. In these gas-conscious times, in an overcrowded world, a scooter makes more sense than ever. Anyone who has ever attempted to park in Downtown, Anywhere, gets the allure of a 2-stroke. And the music? Whether you listen to northern soul, dance floor killers, or Who-inspired riffage or you skank along to classic rock-steady beats, it's all timeless.

Most of the bands have long since split. Apart from the occasional reunion show from bands of the era—most recently the Jetz and Three O'Clock have returned for a few more gigs—just a version of the Untouchables, now only featuring original vocalist Jerry Miller, and Manual Scan, featuring three out of four of the original combo, still perform and record. Of the later bands it's pretty much down to No Doubt and the Bangles who still tour and chart. Of course, Southern

California continues to produce Mod culture with new combos such as the Bassics emerging.

But it will never be the same. Those were more innocent times, when you could still have adventures, when 16-24 year olds could travel to meet other like-minded youths, simply because they shared a love for a look and sound. Music at the time was still considered to be sometimes dangerous, possibly subversive, and certainly influential. Today, great as some music still is, it's too often used as little more than a marketing exercise.

But you only need to do a quick YouTube search to experience visually, in muted detail perhaps, what the excitement was about. Putting on the records brings you closer to the action. It's easy to see that this is an era that's ripe for rediscovery: A unique moment in history when Southern California's surf and sunshine mixed with Britain's Mod look and sounds for an explosion of youth culture that still resonates today.

Bart Mendoza is a San Diego-based journalist, producer, musician, and promoter whose work has appeared in publications such as the San Diego Reader, San Diego Union Tribune, *and* Shindig Magazine. *As a musician he's recorded and toured the world with his bands Manual Scan (the 1980s) and the Shambles (the 1990s). On the business side, he's worked for Diamond Distribution, as well as doing promo for numerous labels including Capitol Records, EMI, Motown, Chrysalis, and Higher Octave. He currently performs with the band True Stories and runs the Blindspot Records label.*

ABOUT THE AUTHOR

Shahriar Fouladi received his Ph.D. in Visual Studies from the University of California in Irvine and has taught courses on film, television, comic books, and more. He is a published author on the superhero phenomenon in film and TV and is the editor of several graphic novels. He works as a writer and editor for a media and entertainment company in Orange County, California. He is currently working on his own superhero comic book series and a science fiction screenplay. He resides in Southern California with his wife Laura, cat Lola, and dog Harvey, who inspired the character of the same name in the book.